The door was closed. I hesitated. M
didn't want to reveal my presen
unconscious, who would answer? That's

I turned the door handle. A chill hit
force it almost knocked me over. Inside, the already jumbled and broken furniture looked as if someone had attacked it with a sledgehammer. Shattered chairs, tables, shards of glass from ruined mirrors, littered the floor. Cupboards had been stacked up so that I couldn't see the back of the room clearly. Charlie could be in amongst this and I wouldn't know. Not unless I went in properly and worked my way through to the back.

Anxious to avoid tripping, I stepped carefully. Some of the debris could provide a deadly weapon to anyone with murder on their mind. Anyone—or anything.

I threw broken chair arms and legs out of the way and heard a crunch of glass under my feet. I looked down and picked up a small silver frame, carefully wiped it and stared at the image. Nathaniel Hargest glared back at me...

THE DEVIL'S SERENADE

CATHERINE CAVENDISH

Copyright © 2016 by Catherine Cavendish
ISBN 978-1-63789-042-4
Macabre Ink is an imprint of Crossroad Press Publishing
All rights reserved. No part of this book may be used or reproduced in any manner whatsoever without written permission except in the case of
brief quotations embodied in critical articles and reviews
For information address Crossroad Press at 141 Brayden Dr., Hertford, NC 27944
www.crossroadpress.com

First Crossroad Press Edition - 2024

Dedication

To Colin, without whom…

and in loving memory of Susan Roebuck—
tragically lost to us far too soon. We miss you, Sue.

Acknowledgments

As always, I am indebted to my friend and fellow horror writer, Julia Kavan, who reads my work, imparts her wisdom and steers me away from the paths of sheer folly. My thanks too to Shehanne Moore, Sue Roebuck, Don D'Auria and all at Crossroad Press.

I hear it at the same time as the others. A sigh, running through the entire fabric of the house.

Hargest has heard him.

And his master is hungry.

Maddie

Chapter One

"In addition to the rewiring and a new boiler, those radiators are way past their sell-by date." Charlie Evans wiped his oily hands on an old rag and pulled the cellar door shut behind him. "I could do a patchwork job, but you might want to consider getting the whole lot done at once. It'll be more efficient and probably work out cheaper in the long run."

I grimaced as I handed him a mug of tea. In my old life a new central heating system would have represented a major financial strain. I still couldn't get used to the fact that I could now afford it without even thinking about it. "When would you be able to do it?"

He set down his mug. "I could start next Monday, if that's good for you."

"Next Monday's fine," I said.

He grinned, showing even white teeth. He smoothed his dark hair, which he wore collar length and neatly trimmed. Even though he was in work clothes, he managed to appear well groomed, despite a morning spent in my dusty cellar.

My cellar. *My* house. Thanks to my Aunt Charlotte, I was now Mrs. Madeleine Chambers of Hargest House, Priory St. Michael. It had a ring to it and a certain grandeur. Pity *Mr.* Chambers—Neil— wouldn't be around to share it. Not for the first time, I gave thanks that our divorce and all financial settlements had been finalized two years earlier. I smiled. He wouldn't see a penny of this. Ever. Not even after my death.

Not that this was a house I would have chosen for myself. Practically every door creaked, and the building's imposing presence could cast a chill over the sunniest day. Constructed from gray stone and brick, its Gothic towers stood four stories high and the tall windows seemed to hide curious eyes and guard dark secrets. This was a house that truly reflected the man who created it.

Nathaniel Hargest was a wealthy industrialist who made his fortune out of mining Welsh slate. He rode his workforce hard. To him it was all about profit and employees were expendable—conditions were deplorable. Mother rarely spoke of him, but one time she told me he made his regular patrols brandishing a bullwhip, and the loud crack it made when he exercised it proved sufficient deterrent to any slacking. Whether he used it on any of his men, she didn't know, but they certainly appeared to have believed him capable of it. I never questioned Aunt Charlotte about him. She seemed reluctant to supply me with even the most basic of details.

Hargest built his house in 1908—as ostentatious as any Gothic revival mansion of the period and set in five acres of largely uncultivated land with a river running through it.

By the time war broke out in 1939, Nathaniel was in his late fifties, a wealthy bachelor, living alone. He had few domestic staff and those he did retain didn't stay long. His temper was meaner than his wages.

Then, in 1955, an attractive twenty-eight-year-old woman named Charlotte Grant came to work as his housekeeper. Local rumor soon grew rife about the true nature of their relationship. In the Welsh border community of Priory St. Michael, the majority of inhabitants attended chapel every Sunday. And most Sundays the gossip was about one subject—Nathaniel Hargest and his bit of fluff.

The old man died in 1970 and a shockwave washed over the good people of the small town when his will was published. He'd left everything to Charlotte.

The Sunday biddies had a field day. Rumors of strange satanic rituals, dating from Hargest's time, now attached themselves to her. A few weeks short of her eighty-eighth birthday, Charlotte died.

And left everything to me.

Close to three million in cash, stocks, and bonds, this massive house and grounds were all mine. It took some getting used to as I'd been living in a one-bedroom rented apartment.

For all her wealth, in her declining years, my aunt had let things slip and it would take a lot of work and considerable investment to get the old place fixed. The plumbing and electrics were archaic and probably unsafe and to fix that, I needed a reliable person.

I took to Charlie the instant he turned up in answer to my phone call for help. There was something comfortable and reassuring about him that inspired my confidence. He seemed familiar somehow, even though we'd only just met, and I sensed that if Charlie told me something, I could rely on his honesty. In the past couple of hours, I'd learned that he was fifty, divorced ten years earlier, and had lived in Priory St. Michael all his life.

He picked up his toolbox off the floor by the cellar door. "If you want to know anything about anything in this town, ask me. Chances are I'll be able to point you in the right direction. I'm sure you'll like it here. We have our drama, but mostly it's a nice, peaceful sort of place." He picked his keys up off the table. "Miss Grant was your aunt, you say?"

I nodded. "Yes. I used to spend my summers with her when I was a child. I loved this old house. So many rooms to play in. A perfect playground for a child…"

A memory stirred. Hairs prickled on the back of my neck. In the summer of my sixteenth year, something happened at Hargest House. Something that existed just out of reach in my mind. Something bad. Whatever it was, my mind blocked it out. I never saw Aunt Charlotte again and never returned to the house. Until now.

Of that last summer, no memories remained. Only gaps and that inexplicable feeling of unease I now experienced afresh. I became conscious of Charlie watching me with a slightly curious expression. I cleared my throat and continued.

"You and I are a similar age, so maybe I saw you round the town back then."

"Quite probably." Charlie seemed about to say something else, but changed his mind. When he spoke again I was sure it wasn't what he had planned to say. "I did a little work for Miss Grant now and again. A partial rewiring, a new strip light in the kitchen, that sort of thing. She kept very much to herself. A very private lady." He frowned. "Right, Mrs. Chambers, I'll see you on Monday. Eight thirty sharp and you'll be having lashings of hot water before you know where you are."

"That'll be super, Charlie. I'm grateful for my power shower but I do love a good wallow in a nice, deep bath. That poor old boiler isn't up to the job. Besides, I really can't be doing with oil. And do call me Maddie, please. 'Mrs. Chambers' makes me think you're talking to my ex-mother-in-law." I raised my eyes heavenward and he laughed.

"You didn't get on, I assume?"

"You assume correctly. She was an absolute witch. Hated me for marrying her son and hated me even more when we split up. I couldn't win."

He opened the front door and hesitated. "Have you been down to your cellar?"

I shook my head. I'd been too busy sorting out the rooms on the first two floors to venture any higher or lower in this vast house. "What's the problem?" A horrific thought hit me. "Oh God, don't tell me I've got rats or mice or...*something*." An image of a horde of cockroaches flashed into my mind, munching their way through anything they could get their disgusting little jaws into.

"No, no, not that I could see anyway. No, it's not that. It's roots."

I blinked. "Roots? What—tree roots or something?"

He nodded. "Yes, you've got some growing down there. You may want to get them dealt with."

"You mean they're coming in under the foundation? But there's no tree close enough for that."

"Nevertheless you have tree roots growing in your cellar. It's certainly odd. I mean, the cellar's a bit damp, but not excessively so." He hesitated, then shook his head.

His wasn't the sort of news I wanted to hear. "Thanks for letting me know," I said as I followed him out to his van. He left with a smile and a wave.

After he'd gone, I stayed outside, looking out over the grounds. In front of me, fifty or so yards away, stood a strangely distorted weeping willow. It had been struck by lightning many years earlier and had grown bent and twisted. The branches hung low and weaved their way across the grass in such a fashion that, as a child, I had christened it "the tentacle tree". From my angle, I couldn't even see the lowest one where I used to sit when I was a child. I had loved that tree, but… Some trace of a hidden memory unnerved me. I had no idea what it was and my mind wasn't letting me anywhere near it, but my hands began to shake. I told myself I was being stupid and turned back into the kitchen.

Once inside, I marched over to the cellar door and opened it. It gave a protesting squeak and I made a mental note to oil the hinges later. Right now I was curious to see this tree phenomenon that so intrigued Charlie.

I had always been possessed of an acute sense of smell. My mother used to comment on it. From what she and everyone else told me over the years, I could detect almost anything way before it reached anyone else's nostrils. With a pleasant aroma, this was a blessing; with a bad one, a curse. Now, my nose wrinkled at the pungent earthy smell—a sharp contrast with the warm, fresh kitchen. I flicked the light switch and a single, weak bulb illuminated part of the expanse stretching out at the bottom of the flight of wooden stairs. I grasped the banister and began my descent. The farther down I went, the stronger the smell of soil, which had taken on a peaty tinge.

A large flashlight rested on the bottom stair and I switched it on, shining it into the dark corners. There wasn't a lot to see. A few broken bits of furniture, old fashioned kitchen chairs, some of which looked vaguely familiar, jam jars, crates that may once have held bottles of beer.

The beam caught the clump of gnarled and twisted roots that intertwined with each other, like Medusa's snakes. I edged closer to it, my heart thumping more than it should. It was only a tree, for heaven's sake! The nearest one was probably the willow. Surely, that was too far away? I knew little about trees, but I was pretty certain their roots couldn't extend *that* far.

I examined the growth from every angle in that silent cellar. The roots were definitely spreading along the floor and, judging by the thickness and appearance of them, had been there for many years. Gray, like thick woody tendrils, they reached around six feet along and possibly four feet across at their widest point. I bent down. Close up, the smell that arose from them was cloyingly sweet. Sickeningly so. I put one hand over my nose, rested the flashlight on the steps and reached out with the fingers of my free hand to touch the nearest root. It wriggled against my palm.

I cried out, staggered backward and fell against the stairs. The flashlight clattered to the floor and went out. Only the overhead bulb provided any light, and it didn't reach this darkest corner. Something rustled. I struggled to my feet, grabbed the torch and ran up the stairs. I slammed the door shut and locked it, leaned against it and tried to slow down my breathing. A marathon runner couldn't have panted more.

I tapped the flashlight and it flickered into life, seemingly none the worse for its accident. I switched it off and set it on the floor by the cellar door. Whoever came to fix those roots was going to need it.

It proved surprisingly difficult to get anyone to sort out my arboreal problem. A steady procession of self-proclaimed tree surgeons, along with gardeners and builders, drifted through my kitchen and back out again, shaking their heads.

Monday came and Charlie rang the doorbell as my mantel clock chimed the half hour. I told him my difficulty, suppressing the need to share my odd experience when I touched the root.

"While I'm down there, I'll take a closer look," he said. "It's probably a bit tricky, but I would have thought at least one of them could have coped with it. Wouldn't they even quote?"

I shook my head. "No. They seemed more intent on getting out of my house and on to their next job." I smiled, but it had struck me as strange how they had all behaved quite casually when they arrived but by the time they left, each seemed a little paler than when they had arrived. None of them wanted to stay and chat. Well, I supposed it wasn't every day you came across a tree intent on growing horizontally rather than reaching for the sky.

Charlie unloaded the new boiler and radiators. He disappeared down the cellar steps armed with a much more powerful set of lights than I possessed. I asked him to fix the lighting down there and install some more bulbs. I wasn't running the risk of any repetition of my earlier experience.

I was clearing away after a sandwich lunch when the doorbell rang. Charlie had taken himself off for a bite to eat so I was alone.

A smart, middle-aged lady with short, black hair, dressed in a black skirt, sensible blouse, and practical shoes smiled cheerily at me on my doorstep. In my old jeans and comfortable, much-worn T-shirt, I felt under-dressed. My recently cut hair was mussed and I tucked it behind my ears. At least my new neighbor didn't seem too shocked at my disheveled appearance, although I could hardly have looked less like anyone's idea of an heiress.

"Hello, I'm your neighbor, Shona Leslie. I wanted to welcome you to Priory St. Michael."

I stepped back to let her in. "Nice to meet you. I'm Maddie Chambers."

"Oh yes, I know who you are." She followed me inside. "Everyone knows who you are. I'm afraid that's small towns for you. They probably knew you'd moved in before you did yourself."

I took to her easy manner instantly. A few minutes later, we settled into my comfortable chairs in Aunt Charlotte's living room, armed with cups of coffee. We had just sat down when the front door opened and closed.

"Charlie's back," I said. The cellar door banged shut, louder than I expected. I jumped.

"Charlie?" Shona asked.

"Evans. I'm having new central heating installed," I said, as my heart beat returned to normal.

Shona nodded and smiled. She kept glancing at my aunt's many pictures of storm-tossed landscapes and dark, bleak moorland that decorated every wall.

"Not my taste, I'm afraid," I said. "I'll get around to sorting all this out over the next few weeks. I can hardly move in this room for all the furniture and knick-knacks. Aunt Charlotte clearly didn't like throwing anything away."

"It's a generational thing, isn't it?" Shona said, setting her coffee mug down on a small table I'd cleared for that purpose. "People of her era covered every surface with photographs."

Shona's voice held no trace of an accent but I instinctively knew she wasn't local. If nothing else, her olive coloring was unusual for this area.

"Have you lived here long?" I asked.

"Not long. I moved into the vicarage when the church sold it a couple of years ago. The town's part of a team ministry these days. A vicar comes over from Rokesby Green to take the services and look after the parishioners. Priory St. Michael used to have their own vicar, but I believe the last one left in rather unusual circumstances. Something happened here about six years ago and it badly affected him."

I sat forward. "Really. What was it?"

Shona hesitated as if she wasn't sure whether or not she should tell me. But I would find out anyway. As soon as I went into the local shop, someone would take great delight in regaling the newcomer with all the gossip.

"In the High Street, up the hill from here, there used to be a social club," she said. "I believe it had been there for decades but about six years ago, a fire broke out one night and destroyed the place. Completely gutted it."

"That must have been awful. Was anyone hurt?"

She shook her head. "Happily, no. A young woman called Suzannah, who worked in the bar, was rumored to have been killed, only they never found her body so it's generally assumed she must have decided to leave. Mind you, some scandalmongers would have it that she started the fire." Shona frowned. "The club steward and his wife were unharmed. They stayed on for a couple of years in a flat over a shop at the top of the hill, but they moved on. I don't know where and I don't know if anyone keeps in touch with them still.

They used to be friendly with Rhiannon Davies, who has something of a local reputation as a witch, but she's moved on as well now. She was the one who called on the vicar to perform an exorcism."

I blinked. "*Exorcism?* Really?"

Shona nodded. "According to local gossip, the club was haunted by some evil spirit and the vicar was called on to get rid of it. The fire could be seen for miles. People said the flames burned blue and green. Unusual to say the least. Maybe it was something in the wood or the paint or something. Anyway, as you might imagine, the more outlandish gossip had it that it was a holy fire, cleansing the evil." Shona struck a dramatic pose, then laughed. "Whatever the truth of it, shortly after that, the poor man's health began to decline. He stuck it out as long as he could but, after several bouts of pneumonia and unexplained viruses, he threw in the towel and took early retirement. I understand he lives in Somerset with his sister."

"Do you believe the gossip?"

Shona shrugged and took a sip of coffee. "I tend to keep an open mind about such things. There's no doubt that the vicar was profoundly affected by what happened that night. Any more than that I really couldn't say, not with any certainty anyway. I'm sure you know the rumors that circulated about your aunt?"

I didn't. "Rumors?"

Shona's eyes widened. "Oh, gosh, I'm sorry. I'm speaking out of turn. I felt sure someone would have filled you in by now. You've been here over a week and it doesn't take them long. Especially as you've got Charlie doing work for you." She smiled. "They say women gossip, but he can give any one of them a run for their money any day of the week."

I smiled. Contrary to what she may have thought, that hadn't been my experience. Still, it was early days. "So what were these rumors?"

"Your aunt grew quite eccentric as she became older. So I believe anyway. She had always lived quietly, but she virtually withdrew from the village. That's when the rumors began. Satanic rites, rituals. Stuff involving that tree as well. You know, the willow."

"The one that was struck by lightning years ago? I call it the tentacle tree because of the weird way it grows."

She laughed. "Good name. Those curvy branches do look like tentacles, don't they? You know you have a public right of way along that path, by the river?"

"Yes, I saw it on the deeds. I remember when I came here as a child I used to see people wandering along there with their dogs. No one seemed to do any harm so I don't think it bothered Aunt Charlotte. But when I knew her she was very laid back anyway. I had some wonderful summers here. She let me do what I pleased. Within reason. The only one I can't remember at all is the last one." Yet again, as I struggled to recall even one tiny detail of those lost weeks, the shutters slammed down in my mind.

"You were lucky to have this place to come to when you were growing up," Shona said. "It must have been wonderful for any child with an imagination. Did your parents come too?"

I shook my head. "They were adventurers. Well, whenever they could be at any rate. My mother was a nurse and my father was an accountant, but they lived for their safaris, following herds of wildebeest and goodness knows what else. They thought it wasn't suitable for a child. Too dangerous. So Aunt Charlotte volunteered and got landed with me every year, until I turned sixteen. After that, I never saw her again. I never came back here until her funeral eight months ago."

"Do your parents still go on their safaris?"

I shook my head. "They were killed in a car crash eleven years ago, on their way back from the airport after a holiday in India, tiger watching or some such thing. A drunk driver pulled out of a side road. They didn't stand a chance. He got two years." I tried to suppress the bitterness and sense of injustice that filled me, even after all these years. I may not have been particularly close to my parents, but they deserved more than for their killer to receive such a light sentence. Two years. One year for each life he took.

"I'm so sorry. Do you have any brothers or sisters?"

Inquisitive. But no doubt she was the advance guard, sent to glean as much information about me as possible to pass on to her neighbors.

"No. Just me. We were a very small family. Now, even smaller. There really is only me these days, since my husband and I divorced."

"Oh dear, I'm sorry to hear that." She took a sip of coffee. "I'm probably the newest resident apart from you. In fact, you coming here means I'm no longer the new kid in town." She smiled. "I'm only a few yards away, over the bridge. You can always talk to me if you're feeling a bit down. It can be difficult, moving to a strange place. Well, not totally strange of course, but it's been—how many years since you were last here?"

"Thirty-two. Thank you, I appreciate that, but I'm fine. Neil and I have been divorced two years, so I did all my grieving then. Now I'm looking forward to doing this place up and deciding what I'm going to do with it. I'd forgotten how massive it is. I've not even been up to the two top floors yet." I suddenly remembered. "Come to think of it, I rarely went up to the top floor as a child either. Except…" Something flashed through my mind. Not detailed enough to be called a memory. Just a feeling. Of blackness. Cold.

I shivered.

There was something in that blackness. Something unnatural.

Something evil.

Chapter Two

March 1611

Charlie came in as Shona was driving off. "Sorry I took so long. Old Mrs. Thomas next door to me collared me when I got home. Her fuses had blown in the middle of cooking her lunch. She's all on her own. Eighty-five years old she is, so I couldn't leave her stranded. As it turned out the job took me longer than I anticipated. Is something wrong?"

I must have looked as perplexed as I felt. "It's just that I heard you come back ages ago, when Shona Leslie was here."

Charlie shook his head and looked at me as if I wasn't quite sane.

"No, I've been gone the best part of two hours."

A sudden fear chilled my spine. "Charlie, would you mind going down into the cellar for me? I think I may have an intruder. I definitely heard the front door open and close, followed by the cellar door banging shut, about half an hour ago. I assumed it was you."

He raised his eyebrows. Now I was sure he thought I was dotty. "No problem," he said and made for the cellar door. I waited at the top of the steps as he scrabbled around in the semi-darkness. Then the brightness from his flashlight cast eerie beams around the shadowy walls and corners. "There's no one here; maybe it was the wind."

"There isn't any. Besides, I know I heard the doors open and close."

He looked up at me from the bottom of the stairs. "There's definitely no one here except me."

If I pursued this, he would be sure I was losing it. As it was, I found his intense gaze uncomfortable. I forced my voice to sound casual. "Okay, Charlie. Thanks. That's a relief anyway."

I shut the door. I must have imagined it. Unless…

My imagination took off on a wild journey. Maybe I did hear someone. They could still be here. They could have crept out of the cellar and gone upstairs while I was preoccupied with Shona's fantastic tales of exorcisms and holy fires. My mouth was so dry I could barely swallow, but I had to find out. I couldn't ask Charlie to go up those stairs. After what he'd told me, he'd think I was—at best—a hysterical female and—at worst—mad. Ask him to explore my house looking for imaginary intruders and it would be all round the town by tea time. No, I must do it. Without a word, I went out into the hall and stared up at the stairs. I certainly wasn't going up there unarmed.

In the old-fashioned coat-stand, Aunt Charlotte had left an impressive collection of ancient umbrellas with fearsome-looking spikes. Some of them would surely be considered deadly weapons these days. I selected the heaviest and gripped it firmly.

I started up the stairs, straining for even the slightest noise. In the distance, Charlie was hammering something in the cellar, but above me? Not a sound.

The floor creaked as I made my way along the first landing. I checked my room first, relieved to find everything as I had left it earlier. I opened the wardrobe and even checked under the bed. Each subsequent room was empty of furniture, except for the one Aunt Charlotte had used. I would have to tackle that one day. Not today though. I closed the door and went into the next room.

This one had a red, patterned carpet that looked familiar. As a child, I had played in here. Alone, except for my imaginary family.

In the absence of real brothers and sisters, I had created for myself a whole family of imaginary siblings. My older brother Tom, eldest sister, Thelma, my slightly older sister, Sonia, and, finally, Veronica—

four years younger than my eight-year-old self. Together we had adventures until Aunt Charlotte called me down to tea.

"Come along, Sonia," I would say, and in my childish mind she would reply, "Coming, Kelly."

Kelly. I don't know where I found that name but I loved it. Somehow it epitomized the confident child I had created in my alter ego. We couldn't have been more different. Kelly could gallop around the garden on her beautiful snow-white mare, Snowbird. I would sit quietly in the corner of the room and read a book about a girl with a pony. Kelly and her brother and sisters could uncover the mystery of the strange old man living all by himself in an eerie mansion. I would read one of my mother's old Enid Blyton stories about the Famous Five or the Secret Seven and their many adventures.

To Aunt Charlotte's amusement, I would natter away to my imaginary siblings while she set the table. Maybe I even asked her to set places for them. I can't remember after all these years, but I do recall chatting to them while she sipped her tea and smiled.

Standing once again in that familiar room, the memories of those happy days brought a smile to my face.

I had a sudden urge to go over to the tall cupboard in the corner. I opened it and smiled. A part of me knew I would find a poster stuck on the inside door. David Cassidy. His flowing hair and fresh complexion captivated so many of us pre-teens in the seventies. I had the biggest crush on him when I was about nine years old. Apart from that, this cupboard was also bare. Had I really taken all my possessions back with me that last time? Or maybe I didn't come in here anymore by the time I was fifteen or sixteen. Again I struggled to remember anything about that last summer, but the steel barriers of my mind remained shut and nothing would surface.

I touched the familiar face of my former idol. He'd had his ups and downs over the years too, like me. Well, maybe not exactly like me. I hadn't battled his problems with DUI and colossal debt. In my case, it had been a total lack of self-confidence which started in my teens and which no one, least of all me, could understand. It had never left me, and sometimes I was scared even of my own shadow. Small wonder that this spooky old house affected me so strongly.

Finished with the lower rooms, I looked up at the staircase. Who knew when someone had last been up there? Maybe months or years ago. No, sooner than that. Aunt Charlotte's estate had been assessed for probate, so someone must have gone up there in the last few months. Or maybe today. My skin prickled.

But I needed to be sure. This was my house. These rooms, stairs, hell, the bricks and mortar of the place were mine. I couldn't be scared of my own home! Besides, much better to go up there in daylight with Charlie on the premises.

I took a deep breath, gripped the umbrella tighter, grasped the banister and began my ascent.

It smelled fusty up there. Unaired. I forced my trepidation down into the pit of my stomach and began opening doors which protested at the violation. I caught my breath at the sight behind one of them. Shrouds of white sheets greeted me. I tweaked the edge of one and it fell off in a cloud of dust, revealing an old grandfather clock with a cracked face, lying on its side. The wood looked worm-eaten and rotten. I couldn't recall it from my childhood, so who knew how long it had been up here, forgotten and decaying?

I threw the sheet back over it and sneezed. I would need to get a house clearance firm in to deal with this lot. More sheets shrouded old chairs with broken legs, worn coverings and further evidence of woodworm. Chipped mirrors, old bedroom furniture. This room had obviously been used as a general dumping ground for the broken and unloved detritus that any home will accumulate over time.

The dust sheets revealed only a couple of familiar pieces. One was a stuffed eagle under a glass dome. I vaguely recalled it standing on the grand piano in the living room. The piano was still down there, but when the bird had fallen out of favor I had no idea. It stared at me through yellow glass eyes. Astonishingly realistic. I shuddered. There was something malevolent in that gaze. A crazy thought struck me for a second. Almost as if the bird were still alive.

An old wind-up gramophone, in an oak cabinet, stood in a corner. The lid was up and a dusty 78 sat on the turntable. I moved closer and peered at the label, brushing it to make out the title. "Serenade in Blue", Glenn Miller and His Orchestra. A veil lifted in my head and a dim memory stirred. The opening strains of that old tune. For such a sweet love song, the first few bars held a darkness in them—almost ominous—before the familiar strains of the melody kicked in. An inexplicable feeling of despair sent my spirits plummeting as I stared at the old record. The familiar His Master's Voice logo of the dog and the phonograph. I imagined it spinning on the record player and felt suddenly cold. I shivered, turned back to the bird and threw the sheet over it. Why should an old Glenn Miller hit have such an extreme effect on me? Crazy! Something stirred in the back of my mind. Tantalizingly close, but just out of reach. I shook myself and hurried out of the room.

None of the other rooms on that floor contained anything more than the odd worn carpet. The remaining cupboards were bare and there were no beds for any intruder to hide under.

Only the uppermost floor remained. At the top of the stairs, a gust of wind hit me and I nearly fell back down again.

I shrieked, but Charlie wouldn't hear me. Not this far away.

Out of the corner of my eye, something moved. A door was open. Something fluttered. A curtain. I swallowed hard. My hands shook as I let go of the banister and stepped forward.

I let out a sigh of relief. The window in the room was open. Thin cotton drapes ruffled in the breeze. I half ran and pulled the sash window closed. The breeze stopped. The drapes stilled.

I closed the last door on the top floor and made my way back downstairs, with still no explanation for what I had heard down there earlier. Maybe that open window created some sort of draft which made a door bang, and I had assumed it was Charlie coming back.

He was emerging from the cellar as I wandered into the kitchen. I smiled at him.

"How's it going?"

"Not bad. Should be finished by Thursday teatime. Are you still sure you only want radiators on the landings of the upper two floors?"

"Yes, for now anyway. I'm not sure what my plans are for up there, so at least those will help keep the place dry and take the chill off."

He nodded. "Any chance of a brew? I'm parched."

"Of course. I'll put the kettle on."

He hovered nearby while I made the tea, as if he wanted to want to say something.

When I thought he'd decided against it, he spoke.

"I've had another look at that tree of yours."

"Any ideas how I'm going to get rid of it?"

"Frankly, no. I mean, I can saw off the roots as far as I can reach, but they'll probably grow back again."

"I'm concerned about the damage to the foundation," I said.

"Didn't you have a survey done?"

I shook my head. "There didn't seem any point. I mean, I intended to live here anyway. I never thought. I suppose if I'd been intending to sell, it might have been different. Maybe that's what I should do. Get a surveyor in."

"Maybe. Or a professional arborist. They understand all about tree growth."

"I had a tree surgeon. Dai Harries."

Charlie snorted. "I've known Dai since he was a snotty-nosed kid. He's not a proper tree surgeon. Not an arborist anyway. Dai's more of a hacker. He chops branches off, fells the odd nuisance tree. You know, the cute little leylandii that grows to monstrous proportions? Then he'll tarmac your drive and repair your fence. He's a proper jack of all trades, our Dai. No, for something like this, you need a specialist. It'll cost you, mind." He hesitated.

"Is there something you're not saying, Charlie? If it's more bad news, I need you to tell me."

"It's just that…well, I know some trees have roots which can extend for maybe three times their total height. Willows, for example. The only tree anywhere near here is that one on the riverbank and, because of what's happened to it, it's difficult to predict how tall it should be, so much of it is lying on the ground. But I can't see how the roots could grow this far. I seem to remember being told that you shouldn't plant willow closer than about fifty feet from a house, but any further than that should be fine."

"Maybe these roots don't belong to that tree at all," I said. Are they even still alive?" I remembered how that root had felt, wriggling in my hand. It was alive all right, however I might wish otherwise. "Maybe there used to be another tree here, closer to the house, and it was chopped down." I hoped Charlie believed this. If he did, there was a chance it could be true and I could suppress the increasing sense of unease inside me.

But all he said was, "Maybe."

The tiny spark of hope in my mind snuffed out. "You don't look convinced."

"It's the way they've come into your cellar. I mean, I've heard of tree roots growing under foundations and cracking up floors and so on, but I can't see how on earth these have got in. It's almost as if they're part of the fabric of the house." He shook his head. "I've never seen anything like it."

The hand holding his mug of tea trembled a little. It disturbed me. Charlie didn't strike me as the nervy type, yet this tree business seemed to have really affected him. Nothing else for it, I had to get this sorted out.

"Do you know any professional arborists at all?"

He blinked. "I'm sorry I don't, but you should be able to find someone online." He set his mug down and looked away—over my shoulder in the direction of the cellar door. I turned to see what had attracted his attention. Nothing there. I looked back. Still avoiding my eyes, he stood. "Ah well, back to what I understand."

After he'd gone back upstairs, I was left with my own thoughts.

Dark thoughts.

Chapter Three

July 1975

Maddie's—so-called—best friend, Diane, frowned at her. "You're mad, you are. You talk to yourself."

"I don't."

"Yes you do. I've heard you. Your lips move. You were doing it just now. You didn't know I was watching."

"That's not true." Lying didn't come naturally to Maddie. She had been talking to—well, not herself exactly—but Diane would never understand. Diane Fraser, with her freckles and her perfect blonde plaits. Diane with her older sister who wore sheer black tights and looked terribly grown up, even though she was only fourteen. But fourteen did seem grown up to nine-year-old Maddie.

Diane looked past Maddie. In the school playground, all the other kids were dashing around, playing games, laughing. The boys were kicking footballs and scoring pretend goals. Diane looked bored. Maddie's spirits plummeted, as they did every time she realized that her best friend didn't understand her.

"It's because you don't have any brothers and sisters," Diane said. She always said that. It was her answer for all Maddie's shortcomings. "I don't know why your mum and dad didn't have any more children. My mum says it's not right to just have the one, and you're the only one in the class who's on her own. All the rest of us have got at least one brother or sister."

Tears welled into Maddie's eyes. She turned away, not wanting Diane to see them. If only she could be more like her imaginary self—Kelly. She wouldn't stand for this nonsense from anyone. *She* would stand up for herself and tell Diane to get lost. But Kelly had a brother and three sisters. Diane wouldn't have taunted her about being an only child.

At home, Maddie's mother wasn't sympathetic.

"What on earth have you two fallen out about now?" she said as she washed up the dishes after dinner and handed them to her daughter for drying.

No way was Maddie going to tell her mother the real reason. That Diane thought she was strange for talking to herself. Mother was always going on at her about that anyway.

"She said I was different because I was the only one in the class who didn't have a brother or a sister. Why don't I have any brothers or sisters?"

"Oh, for heaven's sake. Not *that* again. I've told you before. After I had you I was told I couldn't have any more. Let's not have this conversation again, please. It upsets me."

Maddie opened her mouth to ask another question but shut it again. Mother would get cross. She always did. Maddie handed her the damp tea towel.

"I've finished," she said.

The corners of her mother's mouth twitched in a hint of a smile. "Good girl. Now you can have your treat."

Maddie followed her mother to the tall kitchen cupboard. Her mother reached in and took out a small strawberry-flavored lollipop. Maddie took it from her, eagerly. "Thank you," she said. It would be her only candy that day. Her parents were strict about her sugar intake—another thing Diane teased her about. Never mind though, Maddie would have the last laugh when her friend's teeth all dropped out. And they surely would one day. Mother had said so. Not in so many words, of course. But she said that too much sugar made your teeth rot, and they would all fall out, like Tom the cat's did on the cartoons, when Jerry the mouse hit him in the mouth with a mallet.

Maddie smiled. Diane had such perfect white teeth, but not for long if she kept eating all those Jelly Babies she liked so much. That'd show her!

Maddie's mother rubbed moisturizing lotion into her hands. "Now run along to your room and decide what you would like to take to Aunt Charlotte's. School finishes on Friday and you're going down there on Saturday, so there isn't long if anything needs washing or ironing. Your father and I need to make some final preparations for our safari, so we'll be busy until your bedtime. Make sure you have a bath and brush your teeth and I'll come to tuck you up at nine o'clock. Off you go."

Maddie trotted out of the kitchen and up the stairs to her room. She closed the door and felt the familiar thrill and rush of adrenaline. This was her haven. Her world. In here, she was Kelly—ready to have adventures with her sisters and brother. Right now, they were in the middle of a case. They were staying in an ancient castle and had been exploring the rambling corridors. Last night, Kelly had opened a door into a dimly lit room. They'd just crossed the threshold when Mother had called her for her bath. It was time to discover what lay waiting for them.

First, though, she would have to obey her mother and get out the clothes she wanted to take. None of them would need washing as everything was clean anyway.

Maddie wasn't particularly interested in what she wore. That was another thing she and Diane didn't have in common. In fact, as Maddie opened drawers and took out knickers, short white socks, T-shirts, and shorts, she couldn't think of one interest they did share. Apart from David Cassidy of course. Diane said when she grew up she was going to marry him. She'd become quite upset when Maddie told her he already had a girlfriend. It had been in one of her comics so it must be true. In fact, that was the start of their latest falling out. Maddie sighed, grabbed a handful of dresses out of the wardrobe and plonked them on her bed. She began folding all her clothes and putting them in neat piles on the linen chest that held her bedding. Mother would pick them up, go through them all, and pack a suitcase for her in the next day or two.

On Saturday her parents would drive her the fifty miles or so down to Aunt Charlotte's house, stay for an hour chatting about boring grown-ups' things and then go on to the airport. A little thrill surged through Maddie. This was the second year of staying with her aunt and, if last year was anything to go by, she couldn't wait. At home here she had a tiny garden to play in and Mother was always coming into her room and telling her off.

"Stop talking to yourself, Maddie. People will think you're simple," Mother would say.

Aunt Charlotte's house was so enormous, Maddie could chatter away to her heart's content and never have to worry. Besides, Aunt Charlotte seemed to find it all amusing. She understood. Who cared if Diane Fraser didn't want to be her friend anymore? Maddie had Aunt Charlotte.

Maddie slipped into her cotton nightdress and climbed into bed. She glanced over at the bedside clock. Just before nine. She cuddled down with her toy panda and waited. Mother would be up soon.

At nine twenty, there was still no sign of her mother and Maddie lay wide awake, staring at the ceiling. Maybe if she got herself a glass of water that might help her sleep, but she wasn't supposed to get out of bed except to go to the bathroom. Of course, if Mother had come up when she said she would, she could have brought her the water. Maddie decided that in the circumstances, she couldn't really be in trouble, and scrambled out of bed. She started down the stairs and her parents' voices wafted up to her from the open living room door. All thoughts of water flew out of her mind when she realized what they were talking about. She sat on the stairs, hugging her knees to her chest and listened.

"I'm not really happy about it, Marjorie," her father said. "I can't help thinking that Charlotte could be a bad influence on Maddie. You said yourself she's had a pretty colorful life."

"Only when she was younger," her mother said. "We lost touch for a few years when she went to London and I've no idea what she got up to there. Then our mother died and we met up again at the funeral. Charlotte put willow on her grave for some reason."

"You told me she was into the occult. Ouija boards and all that stuff. I don't want her filling Maddie's head with a load of mumbo jumbo."

My mother laughed. "Oh, she won't do that. That was all a lot of daft stuff she did when she was a child. I'm sure she's over it by now."

"What about that spell book you told me she'd got? Doesn't seem as if she's over it to me."

"Look, don't worry. Anyway, it's not a spell book, it's a Book of Shadows. All perfectly harmless. She writes recipes and poems in there, and she keeps it in a drawer in her bedroom when Maddie's around. Not that it would matter if she found it anyway."

"Well, we'll see how it goes this summer," Maddie's father said. "But the first sign of any weirdness and we'll have to rethink our plans for next year."

Maddie's mother let out a deep sigh. "If she doesn't go to Charlotte's, we won't be able to go on safari. It's as simple as that. The child loves her aunt and the feeling is clearly mutual. She was fine last summer, wasn't she?"

"Well…yes…but she's getting older and takes more in. She understands more."

"She'll be fine. Oh heavens, look at the time! It's after nine thirty. I was supposed to tuck Maddie in at nine!"

Maddie scampered up the stairs and dived into bed. She screwed her eyes shut and didn't open them when her mother tiptoed into her room and kissed her lightly on her forehead.

"Don't go wandering off too far, Maddie. Your dinner will be ready soon."

"No, Aunt Charlotte. I won't." The child stared up at her aunt and blinked her clear brown eyes. She glanced over her shoulder. "Come on, Sonia. Let's go upstairs and play in our room."

Maddie skipped out of the kitchen, into the hall. Her Aunt Charlotte smiled, shook her head, and returned to her beef casserole.

On the second floor, Maddie reached up to the door handle. This one was stiffer than the others and she needed all her strength to turn it. The tip of her tongue protruded from her lips as she put all her concentration and both hands into her task. She felt the catch give and smiled in triumph.

Again, she looked over her shoulder. "Come on. Let's play!"

Coming.

Maddie hopped and skipped to the far side of the room and opened the cupboard door. She stepped back just in time to miss a heap of board games and books spilling out onto the floor. She put her hands on her hips as she had seen her mother do countless times when admonishing her daughter for the state of her bedroom.

"Oh dear, Sonia. Looks like Veronica's been naughty. We shall have to punish her."

We'd best tell Thelma. She's the oldest. It's her job to tell her off.

"You're right. Where's she got to?"

Probably gone out. Buying makeup. Or a new dress.

"I expect so." Maddie sighed. "Oh well, I suppose I'll have to put everything back. Aunt Charlotte will be cross if she sees all this."

I'll help you, Kelly.

"Thank you, Sonia."

Invisible friends were all well and good, but when it came to clearing up messes, they weren't much help. Maddie did her best, accompanied by a lot of sighing and tutting. Cluedo was stacked on top of Spirograph, on top of Monopoly, on top of Bunty and Tammy Annuals for Girls.

Maddie smoothed her dress and stepped back to admire her handiwork. "There," she said, in a near perfect imitation of Aunt Charlotte. "All shipshape again."

She knelt down and took a few seconds to flick through the pages of *The Book of Strange Stories*, which she had perched precariously on the top of the uncertain pile. She found it. Her favorite story. All about a Siamese cat who helped to solve a mystery. Of course this cat wasn't like the aloof Siamese her mother's friend, Mrs. Walters, had. Her cat, Simba, always licked his paw and sped out of the room whenever Maddie went near him. She wondered if he had any adventures or solved any mysteries. She also wondered what it would be like to have a cat of her own. Or a dog maybe.

"Mother won't let us," she said out loud. "She says she would have to look after it and she doesn't have time. I keep telling her I'd take care of it, but she doesn't believe me. It's not fair." Tears filled her eyes and she wiped them away with the back of her hand.

Never mind, Kelly. You've got us. We'll never leave you.

Maddie sniffed and managed a wobbly smile. "Thank you, Sonia. You're all my best friends in the whole world."

"Maddie! Dinner's on the table!" The voice drifted up from far away downstairs.

"Come on, I'm starving!"

Downstairs, Aunt Charlotte was dishing up in the kitchen. The comforting, rich smell of beef casserole made Maddie's tummy rumble. Outside the sun shone during one of the hottest summers on record but inside this house was always chilly. Sometimes Aunt Charlotte even had to light a fire in the evenings, despite the season, so—while everyone around them might be eating salads and praying for rain—inside Hargest House, Charlotte Grant and her niece found a warming casserole more appropriate fare.

Maddie clambered onto her chair. Her feet always dangled and she swung them for something to do while she waited for her aunt to spoon the steaming casserole onto her plate and add fluffy mashed potatoes, and green beans fresh from the garden.

"There you are. Now eat it all up. That's a good girl."

"Thank you, Aunt Charlotte. Can Sonia have some?"

"Yes, of course," Aunt Charlotte said, and proceeded to pile an imaginary plate with invisible food. "There you are, Sonia," she said, setting the "plate" in front of an empty chair.

Thank you.

"Sonia says 'thank you'," Maddie said between mouthfuls of food. The meat was so tender, it melted in her mouth. Not that she would ever say so to her mother, but Aunt Charlotte was a much better cook. She enjoyed working in the kitchen and especially when it meant she could cook something she had grown herself—like the green beans.

They had so much more flavor than any of the frozen supermarket variety Maddie's mother served up at home.

"Have you had a nice day?" Aunt Charlotte asked. "What did you get up to?"

Maddie swung her legs backward and forward as she recalled her activities since the morning.

"I went down to the tentacle tree and I met a nice boy. I think he's a bit older than me. We played 'I Spy' and he showed me how to skim stones on the river."

"That sounds nice. I hope you didn't get too close to the edge though."

Maddie gave Aunt Charlotte what she hoped was a "withering" look. She'd read about someone giving a parent such a look once and she'd always wanted to have an opportunity to practice it. Unfortunately, as Aunt Charlotte merely smiled and gave a little cough, Maddie didn't think she'd managed the desired effect. In fact, she could have sworn her aunt was suppressing a giggle.

"What was this boy's name?" Aunt Charlotte asked. "Maybe I know him."

"Um." Maddie thought but, try as she might, she couldn't remember it or recall if he'd even told her. "I don't know," she said, her eyes downcast.

"Never mind," Aunt Charlotte said. "If you see him again, you can ask him. There are quite a few children around your age in the town. It'll be nice if you can make friends for the summer. Your mother said she's a bit concerned that you always seem to be on your own. You never bring any school friends home."

Maddie looked down at her plate and concentrated on spearing a piece of carrot followed by a small chunk of meat. She raised her fork and filled her mouth. That way she didn't have to answer her aunt. After all, mustn't talk with your mouth full. She could feel Aunt Charlotte's steady gaze, but kept on chewing, longer than necessary. Her aunt sighed and carried on eating. Maddie swallowed.

Maddie didn't want to talk about her recent falling-out with Diane. Besides, her sometime friend had only been to Maddie's house once and then all she'd done was complain about how cold it was.

"Don't you even have central heating?" she had said, holding herself and shivering with exaggerated effect.

"Yes, of course we do," Maddie said, feeling a strong urge to slap her. "But my mother doesn't like it turned up too high. She says it's unhealthy."

"I bet it's 'cause your parents are poor."

"They're *not* poor and you're not to say things like that."

Diane stopped shivering and sniffed. "I'll say what I like. You can't stop me."

After that, Maddie vowed she would never bring anyone home again. Especially when Diane started telling all their classmates about her friend's freezing cold house and Spartan conditions. The other children pitied her. Maddie could read it in their eyes and cried herself to sleep that night. It wouldn't be the last time.

No doubt Diane would complain about Hargest House too if she came there. Not that Maddie would ever invite her. This was *her* special place.

It was simpler to keep the other children away. If no one came home with her, they'd have nothing to talk about. It was true that there weren't many luxuries at home. No fancy freezers or color televisions in every room. Maddie kept pulling threads out of the battered sofa and catching her toe in that threadbare bit of the carpet in her bedroom. They couldn't be poor though. Not *really* poor, because there was always money for her parents' safaris, and she never went hungry, even if the food was a bit plain and basic. Not like this delicious casserole. Maddie's mother bought the cheapest cuts of meat and there was always some gristle and chewy fat spoiling the meal. Aunt Charlotte bought only tender cuts, from the butcher up the road.

Maddie savored every mouthful. If only she could stay with Aunt Charlotte all the time. Maybe she'd become good friends with the boy she met today. If only he'd told her his name.

The next day, rain lashed the windows. There would be no return trip to the tentacle tree today. Instead, Kelly and her brother and sisters could have an adventure. Maddie had been saving an extra special one for just such an occasion.

She had never ventured up to the top floor. Whenever she had peered up the staircase, it always seemed darker and gloomier than any of the other floors. Today though, Kelly would lead the way on a voyage of discovery.

Maddie felt a little thrill zip up her spine as she put her foot on the first tread of the staircase.

It's awfully dark up there.

"Don't worry, Veronica. I'll protect you, and Tom's got his blunderbuss."

Maddie had no idea what a blunderbuss was, but it had featured in one of her books and sounded quite grand and bold when it was wielded by the hero.

The top floor turned out to be much like the others. Corridors left and right with closed doors. It was silent up there and smelled faintly of dust and beeswax. With her imaginary family behind her, Maddie tried the handle of the first door she came to. It turned smoothly enough and she peered around the door. Empty.

"There's nothing in here. Let's try the next one."

The third room she tried looked more promising. A long, low table lay at one end of the uncarpeted floor. At each corner, huge black candles in wrought iron holders caught Maddie's attention.

"I've never seen black candles before. How strange."

Maddie touched one of them. A sudden rush of wind blew her hair and a pungent smell like rotten eggs made her gag. Goosebumps broke out on her arms. In the far corner a dark shadow moved. Red eyes flashed. Maddie screamed and raced to the door. She tugged at the handle. It wouldn't move. Behind her someone laughed. One massive wrench and the door opened so fast it threw her backward. She recovered her balance and dashed out into the corridor. The door slammed behind her. Maddie ran screaming down the stairs to be met by an anxious Aunt Charlotte in the hall.

"Maddie, whatever's happened?"

Maddie clung to her aunt, sobbing. "Something on the top floor. It was horrible!"

Aunt Charlotte clutched her tightly. "What did you see? Tell me."

Maddie choked back sobs. "A black shadow…it moved…it had red eyes…and a horrible smell."

Aunt Charlotte steered her into the kitchen. "It's all right, Maddie. It's over now." Maddie couldn't stop shivering. When she closed her eyes all she saw was that shadow, staring at her.

"What was it, Aunt?"

Aunt Charlotte sat her niece down on a kitchen chair and took her hands in hers. "It was nothing, Maddie. You've had nightmares before, haven't you?"

Maddie nodded. "But I was asleep then, and it was nighttime."

"Yes, but there are day-mares as well. You don't have to be asleep for those and that's what you've just had."

"It frightened me."

"I'm sure it did, Maddie. That top floor is never used these days, so probably just as well not to go up there again. When rooms are shut up for a long time, they can become very spooky indeed."

Maddie stared at her aunt. "Are you sure there's nothing nasty up there?"

Aunt Charlotte smiled and made a cross over her heart with her finger. "Promise. It was just a day-mare. You'll stop having them as you grow older."

Maddie wanted to believe her with all her heart. "I've never had one before."

"There's a first time for everything and those empty rooms upstairs are just the thing to set your mind racing. Now, how about a slice of my homemade ginger cake?"

Maddie loved ginger cake. Especially Aunt Charlotte's. She nodded, wiped her eyes and blew her nose on the hankie her aunt gave her. She'd had a day-mare. Bet Diane Fraser hadn't had one of those.

After dinner, Maddie dried up the dishes her aunt handed to her and placed them carefully back on their correct shelves in the cupboards.

She took great care to polish the silver knives and forks and the tumblers which had held their drinking water.

Aunt Charlotte emptied the washing-up bowl and wiped down the draining board. She wrung out the dishcloth and laid it across the faucets.

"Shall we play some music and sing this evening, Maddie? Would you like that?"

Maddie, who had been feeling awkward since the unwelcome question about her schoolfriends, grinned. Her spirits shot up from the soles of her feet.

"Oh yes, please."

Aunt Charlotte's face lit up in a brilliant smile that made her eyes shine. She pushed a stray hair back over her ear and grasped Maddie's hand.

"Right, come along. Let's go."

Maddie giggled as she and her aunt skipped out of the kitchen, across the hall and into the living room, right up to the concert grand piano. Her giggles stopped as she caught sight of the stuffed eagle in its glass dome. She flinched from the evil gaze, certain she could see nasty little imps in that fixed stare. It reminded her of a similar creature in one of the tales she had read in *The Book of Strange Stories*. It was the only one that had given her nightmares, but those were real doozies. In them she dreamed a huge owl with golden eyes was coming to get her. She could hear the beating of its massive, flapping wings as it came ever closer, claws outstretched ready to pounce and carry her off.

"Oh, I'm sorry, Maddie. I forgot you don't like Oswald. I'll move him right away." Aunt Charlotte picked up the glass dome and carted the creature out of the room. The stairs creaked as her aunt ascended, no doubt to deposit her burden in one of the upstairs rooms Maddie never ventured into.

While she waited, Maddie wandered over to the bureau and picked up a black and white photograph in a silver frame—one of many that covered the surface. She peered at it closely. There was Aunt Charlotte, looking a few years younger and wearing old-fashioned clothes, with her hair all piled up. She was seated next to a small table on which lay a vase of roses and another photograph. This was of a man. Maddie tried to make out his features. He was wearing a top hat. Like the photograph she had seen of her long dead great-grandfather. The picture was so tiny it was difficult to make out much more, but Maddie's fingers went numb and she bit her lip. She had to concentrate hard not to drop the frame as her fingers throbbed with cold.

She just managed to replace the picture back on the bureau when her aunt returned. Maddie said nothing about what had happened. Maybe she had imagined it. This was a cold house, after all.

Aunt Charlotte made straight for the piano and sat on the stool. She flicked through some sheet music.

"Now what shall we sing today?"

Maddie's eyes lit up. "I like 'Save Your Kisses for Me' by Brotherhood of Man. Can you play it?" She stood at the corner of the piano facing her aunt.

"Oh, I don't think it's too hard. Let's try, shall we? Do you know the words?"

Maddie nodded, her ponytail bobbing.

Aunt Charlotte played the first few notes, hesitant at first, then warming to the simple song. Maddie came in on cue, her childish voice a little off-key but making up for it by enthusiasm and volume.

Half an hour and a dozen songs later, Charlotte called a halt. "It's past your bedtime, young lady, and your mother will have serious words with me if she comes back from Kenya and finds you with big, black circles under your eyes."

"Oh, *please*, Aunt Charlotte. Just one more."

"Oh… Very well. One. But don't tell your mother." Aunt Charlotte put her finger to her lips. "It'll be our little secret."

Maddie nodded. She'd already lost count of how many little secrets the two of them had accumulated that summer and she'd only been there a few days.

Aunt Charlotte began to play some chords. Deep, rumbling chords. Maddie shivered. This was unlike her aunt whose preferred music was usually light and jolly.

"This is a special song. My favorite, from a long time ago. Once upon a time I played it for someone I was very much in love with, and he loved it too. But..." Her voice tailed off and she shrugged her shoulders, as she carried on playing, picking up the melody which became more tuneful, so that Maddie could hum along with it even though it was the first time she had ever heard it.

"That's nice. What's it called?" Maddie asked.

"'Serenade in Blue'. It's by Glenn Miller. You remember, we've played some of his songs. 'Chattanooga Choo Choo' and 'Pennsylvania 65000'."

Maddie nodded. "I remember. I like him. Even though he is old-fashioned."

Aunt Charlotte laughed and began to sing.

A chill shrouded Maddie and she gasped at the suddenness of it. Aunt Charlotte seemed unaware and carried on playing.

Maddie fainted.

Chapter Four

The present

Friday. My central heating worked. I had shiny new radiators and, for the first time, two floors of Aunt Charlotte's house felt warm and toasty. The sun shone on a bright, warm, late September morning and I decided to explore my grounds for the first time since I moved in. First on my agenda was the willow tree.

I started off by the wall of the house, where I estimated the intrusive roots must be. A gravel path ran right around the building and expanded out into a sweeping—if short—driveway, out front, where my little red Suzuki was parked. I bent down, searching for any telltale cracks near the wall of the house. Nothing. The roots hadn't broken up the surface either. But, I thought they generally went no more than a foot or so downward, which was why they caused so many problems with roads and sidewalks—and people's houses.

Since talking to Charlie, I had checked out a few facts. Willows were indeed deemed safe to be planted fifty feet or more away from a building. I stared across the expanse of green between me and the tree. How was it possible that its roots had grown so far down and so far along? There had to be another tree. Or the remains of one, at least. I examined every inch of grass between the house and the tree. Nothing. Nor any remains of a tree stump, although I did discover that the willow was in a direct line with where the roots were appearing.

Determined to conquer my inexplicable aversion to it, I touched the tree. The gnarled bark looked knotted in parts and, in others, wrinkled and even stripped away. The center of the massive trunk was half hollowed out, scorched and withered from the lightning strike that no one could remember even when I was a child. Thick branches curved downward, interweaving with each other, some striking upward, others merely inches off the ground; one or two lay almost flat. It was a miracle tree in some ways. With such awful damage, it really should have died, but its will to live had proved too strong for that.

Feeling confident I had overcome my irrational fear, I sat on the longest branch. It took my weight easily, not creaking or bending. It had spawned its own branches which grew horizontally, entwined with each other and disappeared into the lush undergrowth behind the tree. Indian mallow and clinging ivy grew here in profusion. Nearby, the busy river rushed along, lying low thanks to the dry weather that had persisted for some weeks. But that river could transform into a raging torrent in storm conditions when too much rainwater drained off the mountains to the east. Hargest House had never been flooded; it lay just high enough to escape. Other properties in the town had not been so fortunate, or so Aunt Charlotte had told me.

I stood and took a few paces away from the tree to look at the river. It sparkled in the sunlight, the stones on its bed protruding above the surface. Not a soul was around, even though this was the public walkway. The children would all be at school and their parents working, no doubt.

I sat back down on my branch and gazed upward at the canopy of leaves, now starting to turn autumn yellow. In the light breeze, some fluttered to the ground. Birdsong filled the air from the finches, sparrows, blue tits, and pied wagtails that frequented the area. The busy little town barely intruded on the rural surroundings. Peace and tranquility ruled here.

I placed my hands either side of me, feeling the rough bark. Breathing in the country air, I closed my eyes, to better absorb the gentle atmosphere. But, in a few minutes, my peace was shattered.

It started as a ripple that echoed through my entire body. Then it surged. I gasped, jumped up and stared down at the branch. It wasn't moving, but I had felt it. A strong, rising energy that had coursed through the tree and shot through me like a bolt of electricity.

I don't know how long I stared. I don't know what I expected it to do. Move? I told myself I'd imagined it. It must be the wind, ruffling the leaves, the branches, anything. But there wasn't *enough* wind. The leaves barely stirred.

Finally, I plucked up courage to touch the tree. The bark roughed my fingers; nothing else. Whatever I experienced had stopped. If it had ever even begun.

Once again, a shutter crashed down in my mind. I knew there was something there. Something I should remember. And whatever it was concerned not only the house but also this tree. I had to discover what it was. Even though the thought of what might lay there absolutely terrified me.

"I hope you don't mind me coming round again, but I don't have your phone number, otherwise I would have called."

Shona smiled at me in such a way I knew she had a favor to ask. Never mind, I liked her, had some time on my hands, and needed to get to know my neighbors.

I ushered her into the living room. She gazed around, a smile lighting up her face.

"My goodness, you've made some improvements already. I like it."

I smiled. I was pleased with the room too. It had been so cluttered and dated before. Now, you could actually see some of the surfaces, unfettered by so many photos and ornaments. Not that I'd removed every trace of Aunt Charlotte. I'd left some of her pieces out. The odd small vase and one or two attractive and valuable Chinese ornaments. The walls looked fresh and clean, revitalized by a couple of coats of paint. I'd changed the color scheme from dull and drab faded cream to a subtle antique gold on the walls, a warm butter shade for the ceiling, and paintwork in a color called White Chocolate—not as startling as plain white. One or two of my aunt's favored landscapes remained on the walls, more as a memento of her than for any aesthetic reasons.

"Did you get Charlie's brother in to do the decorating?" Shona asked. "I've heard he's very good."

"I don't think Charlie would have done any more work for me if I'd gone to anyone else. Yes, I thought I'd try him out in here and if he did a good job, gradually get the whole house done. Well the bottom two floors anyway. I still haven't decided on the top ones. I'm wondering about looking at some kind of conversion job. Maybe turn them into flats or something. At least they'd be lived in."

"Sounds like a good idea. There's a shortage of places to rent around here. I don't know if you've heard, but they're knocking that block of flats down in the High Street where the club was."

"Really? But they can't have been up more than a few years."

"About five, I think. They can't get anyone to stay long and now people are refusing to go there at all. The land belongs to a property developer who bought it for a song after the fire. It's losing him money, so down it comes. Terrible waste."

"But why won't people live there? Are there structural problems?"

"Not that I know of. No, it's people's imaginations running riot. They say the evil spirits are still there. Residents have reported seeing a big black dog with flaming red eyes. Some say they've seen it in their flats. Others have said they've been attacked. If you ask me, some people watch too much late-night horror on TV."

I thought back to my experience with the willow. I wanted to share it with someone, but if I told Shona about it, she'd probably think I was also watching too much late night horror.

"You said you'd heard rumors of my aunt and satanic rituals involving the willow tree."

Her eyebrows raised a little, and my confidence sapped. Still, I'd started, so… "What exactly did you hear?"

Shona sighed. "You realize this is all a lot of overblown nonsense? These stories start, goodness knows where, and become embellished the more they are repeated. Each person adds their own little twist, so the story becomes more and more fantastic."

"Nevertheless, I'd really like to hear what people have been saying. Maybe it will help in my dealings with them. For all I know, perhaps they think I'm a devil worshipper as well."

Shona laughed. "Hardly."

But there was something about her laugh that didn't ring quite true. It disturbed me, but I hadn't a clue why. Nevertheless, my skin prickled.

"You're aware your aunt became reclusive in her later years?"

"So I believe. She became housebound and crippled with arthritis."

"Yes, that would explain it. No one saw her. Well, only from a distance, if they were walking along by the river and she happened to be sitting out in her garden, or, more likely, at the bay window in this room or her bedroom. She would sit for hours, her black shawl wrapped around her, staring out, never moving. There were even rumors that she'd died and was a mummified corpse. You know, like Norman Bates's mother in *Psycho*."

I recoiled. "That's pretty gruesome of them." My neighbors tumbled in my estimation.

Poor Aunt Charlotte. She really didn't deserve that kind of treatment.

"But that's precisely what I mean," Shona said. "Someone behaves in a slightly eccentric fashion and the rumor mill cranks up. Anyway, her nurses and care staff came and went. She got through a fair few of them until she switched agencies. A new bunch—two for daytime and two for nighttime—appeared a year or so before she died. The tongues soon started wagging again. These new people didn't fit in at all with the Priory St. Michael way of doing things. Her previous staff used to be seen around the town. A couple of them actually lived around here. But this lot kept themselves very much to themselves. No one even knew their names. One night, Dai Harries saw some lights down by the river. He swears to this day he hadn't been drinking, but it was around midnight, and he says he stood on the bridge and watched these people indulging in some sort of ritual. They were dancing around the tree." She grinned. "More likely, the whisky he'd been drinking was dancing around his stomach, putting fanciful thoughts in his head."

I smiled. My brief encounter with Dai Harries flashed back into my mind. A short, stumpy little man with wispy gray hair and a persistent twitch. I recalled his bulbous, reddish-purple nose. Now I knew the probable reason for it. "But is that it? Nobody has reported anything else happening with the tree?"

"Oh yes, plenty of tales of similar things happening at various times of the year. One woman swore she'd seen the tree dancing. I mean, really!"

"I suppose that's the local equivalent of the stories about the standing stones in Oxfordshire. The ones they call the Rollright Stones are supposed to dance at some time of the year. Halloween I think."

"Yes, I've heard of that." Shona broke eye contact and seemed to be looking at something behind me. I almost turned to see what had grabbed her attention, but she spoke again.

"Anyway, enough of all that nonsense, I've come to ask if you'll do our local Am Dram Society a massive favor."

"What's that?"

"Do you like theater at all?"

"I don't go very often, but I do enjoy a good play." My mind traveled back to enjoyable nights out with Neil. We had supported our local Amateur Dramatic Societies and had also enjoyed going into the city to watch the latest musical, comedy or drama. I couldn't remember the last time I'd sat in the stalls, eyes riveted on the stage.

"We've recently lost our rehearsal room. We were using the Baptist church hall at the top of the town, but the building is being demolished. It wasn't really suitable anyway. Terribly damp and cold in the winter."

"How can I help?"

"Well I was wondering…we were wondering…would you have any room for us to rehearse here? We're amateurs, but we do work hard and take it all very seriously. We'd be no trouble."

It might be fun. And I certainly had the space. "Why not? How many of you are there?"

"Usually between four, and ten or eleven, depending on the play of course. There's the director, prompt and props people, so no more than, say, fifteen."

"No problem. You could use rooms on the second floor. They're mostly empty, so you can have free rein to set up whatever you want in terms of scenery and props. There's a radiator on the landing, but you'll probably need more heating in the colder months. I'll get hold of some portable heaters. As long as you tell me when your rehearsal schedule is, I can switch them on and make sure the room's nice and warm for you. What sort of plays do you put on?"

"Oh, comedies, mysteries. We did Neil Simon's *Plaza Suite* last year. And *Noises Off*. Do you know it?"

I recalled a warm spring evening. Neil and I laughing as we emerged from the local cinema, arm in arm. Good times—before she ruined it all. An inward, silent sigh dampened my mood, but Shona was waiting for an answer and staring at me in a way that made me uncomfortable, as if she could see into my mind and read my dark thoughts. "I've seen the film," I said, and the discomforting gaze morphed into a smile and a nod.

"The play's much better. I think it missed something in the translation to the big screen. We had to put on an extra performance of our production. It was so popular."

"Where do you perform?"

"At the Little Theatre in Rokesby Green, about four miles away. Our next production's an Agatha Christie. *The Murder at the Vicarage*. As I live in the old vicarage, they all thought it'd be quite a hoot if I played the vicar's wife—Griselda Clement. How could I refuse?" She laughed. "We had a read-through at my house last Tuesday, but there isn't enough room there to set up a stage—even an imaginary one— and no one has anything larger."

I sat back in my chair. The more I thought about this idea, the more I liked it. I'd never had the confidence myself to tread the boards but the thought of having a bunch of my neighbors trooping in and out agreed with me. Besides, it was about time I started meeting people and making friends. With my shyness, I never found that easy, but I did have my fallback coping mechanism to help me. It had been a long time since I'd needed her.

"I assume you have an interval while you're rehearsing? I could make tea and coffee. Biscuits maybe?"

"Oh, we couldn't impose on you for that, and I'm afraid we can't afford to pay much rent either. These productions are a lot of fun, and a lot of hard work too, but they barely cover their costs, even though we usually have very good houses. It's the rent of the Little Theatre, you see."

"I'm not charging you. It'll be a pleasure. And, besides, you've solved the problem of what to do with the second floor."

Shona stared at me, her mouth slightly open. "Oh, that is so generous of you, Maddie. The society will be thrilled. Thank you so much."

"My pleasure." I didn't tell her I was already planning to bake a lemon drizzle cake. Neil's favorite. I hadn't made it since he left. Come to think of it, I hadn't baked anything since we split up. Memories of fresh bread, roasting meat, and biscuits hot from the oven floated back. I had spent hours in the kitchen when we were married; when I was happy in my ignorance of Neil's infidelity. Afterwards, I no longer had the heart for it.

The house felt empty when Shona went home. Perhaps I should think about hiring a live-in housekeeper. At least then, at night, when the lights were off, timbers creaked, and the shadows lengthened, I wouldn't be alone. But what would she do all day? When I'd worked in the bookshop, I'd been too busy to bother with any real hobbies, other than reading and following my favorite soaps on TV. But now? Maybe it wasn't a housekeeper I needed at all. A companion. I shuddered at the thought. Companions were for old, lonely, sad spinsters. I was none of those.

As I settled down in front of the television, I looked forward to the theater group's rehearsal nights. Maybe it would also stop my stupid fears of the upper floors.

I was watching some inane sitcom on TV when the doorbell sounded. I glanced at the clock. Eight thirty. I wasn't expecting anyone, but I was quickly learning that, in a place like Priory St. Michael, that didn't really count for anything. People had a habit of turning up, unannounced and uninvited. They'd probably even tried the door handle first to see if it was open. If it had been, they would have wandered in and thought nothing of it. But I'd spent too long living in a city to be so trusting of my fellow residents.

I opened the door and stared at the familiar, but unusually disheveled figure on the doorstep. His shirt was creased, his graying hair had grown long over his collar and he looked like he hadn't shaved in days. When he spoke, he seemed to struggle to raise the hint of a smile, and his feeble effort stopped at the corners of his mouth. His eyes had lost their former sparkle and he seemed to have aged a decade, not a mere three years.

"Hello, Maddie. Long time, no see."

"Neil. What are you doing here?"

"Oh, come on, aren't you going to let me in? Aren't you the least bit curious as to why I've come all this way?"

He took a step forward and I barred his way. "You can say anything you want to say to me on the doorstep, and then you can leave. I told you last time. I never want to see or hear from you ever again."

His expression changed and he wore that hang-dog puppy look that used to work with me years ago. Waves of anger were about to breach the flood barriers in my mind. "And you can cut that out as well."

Predictably, he turned on the wide-eyed innocence that generally preceded a lie. "Cut what out?"

I sighed and folded my arms. "What do you want, Neil?"

"I want to talk to you. That's all. I have something to tell you that I can't say over the phone. I promise I won't outstay my welcome."

"You already have."

Were those actually tears in his eyes? I didn't expect that.

"Maddie, I really need to talk to you. It's important. Do you honestly think I'd put myself through this if it wasn't? I knew what reaction I'd get coming here after what I did to you."

The nerve of the man! "You betrayed me. Liz was my best friend. At least, I thought she was. No one could be anyone's best friend and do what she did, for ten years."

"I know. I know. You have every right to hate me. Us. But please, Maddie, give me ten minutes and I'll be gone."

I hesitated. He did seem genuine. But he had always been a consummate liar. The problem was I hadn't realized that for the first seventeen years of our marriage.

Oh, what the hell? We'd both moved on. I'd achieved the ultimate revenge after all. I had all this. I could give him ten minutes of my life. For old times' sake. I stepped back and let him in.

"Thank you, Maddie. I appreciate this. I can't tell you how much."

I showed him into the living room and went over to the drinks cabinet where I selected a bottle of brandy and two glasses. I unscrewed the bottle and poured two generous measures.

Neil sat down on the settee. He patted the cushion next to him. "I remember this suite from our old house."

"It's about the only thing I brought. You had the rest of the good stuff."

"Only half, Maddie. As we agreed."

"Yes, but I don't remember agreeing to you coming into the house when I wasn't there and cherry picking all the best furniture. No doubt with a little help from Liz. I came home from work to find the place ransacked. I thought at first I'd had burglars. Then I found your note. Cryptic, wasn't it? 'Sorry to have missed you. Regards, Neil.' You knew bloody well which days I worked. You knew the telephone number. You could have called and made an appointment, but if you'd done that, Liz wouldn't have had the pick of the place, would she? That wouldn't have suited her at all. I noticed all the things of mine she had admired over the years somehow managed to make their way into your new flat. I saw them all in those cheesy photos of the pair of you that you kept putting up on Facebook for all the world to see. How is the *dear girl* anyway?" I took a gulp of brandy, refilled my glass and handed the other to my ex-husband. I knew my sarcasm wouldn't be wasted on him.

He took the glass without a word and drained it in one. "Any more where that came from?"

That took me aback. "You don't usually drink when you drive, and I assume you didn't walk all the way from Chester."

He didn't respond. I didn't refill his glass and sat down on my usual chair.

He took a deep breath. "Liz and I split up six months ago." He was certainly full of surprises this evening. "I guess the relationship had run its course. We were arguing all the time and she found someone else…" His voice tailed off. "It was an amicable split."

I didn't ask how much of my furniture she now possessed. "So where are you living then? Still in the same place?"

He shook his head. "I moved. She's buying me out and I'm renting a small flat near where we used to live. Gladstone Street. Do you remember it?"

A vague memory of a collection of streets all named after prime ministers, from Walpole to Baldwin, sprang to mind. Row upon row of small pre-war terraced houses. His place must be quite tiny. At least I'd been able to afford to rent an apartment in a decent part of the city after our house had been sold and we'd split the proceeds. A ripple of sympathy trickled into my brain, only to be stopped in its flow by recollections of lies, deceit, and a harsh divorce settlement that left him winning as much as it consigned me to the loser's bin. I remembered the look of triumph on Liz's face. She had come away with everything she wanted. Not only my property, but my husband as well. It was so predictable, I supposed.

I sipped my second drink, while Neil kept clenching and unclenching his hands. He looked so wretched, I almost relented and poured him another. But no way would I be responsible for him driving over the limit. As it was, he would probably have to stay at least an hour to wear off the effects of the first one. Damn my stupidity. Was he angling to spend the night? Probably. Well, tough shit.

I stood up. "I'll make you a coffee." I left the room before he could protest.

When I returned, he had recovered his composure, at least a little, and was examining one of the few pieces of Aunt Charlotte's porcelain that hadn't been consigned to a box upstairs. A pretty and valuable little bottle.

He replaced it carefully on the mantelpiece. I cringed and wished I'd put it away. But I didn't know *he* was coming, did I?

"It's eighteenth-century," I said. "A handmade Chinese snuff bottle."

He whistled. "Must be worth a few quid. What do these go for now? Five, ten thousand pounds in such good condition?"

My heart jumped. From someone else that might have been a casual remark, but from Neil... I knew him too well. "You know, you had me almost feeling sorry for you," I said, handing him his coffee and concentrating hard on preventing my hand from shaking. My anger had reached boiling point, but no way would I allow myself to lose control. Not tonight. There had been too many screaming matches in the past, and I never won any of them. "You haven't changed. You still know the cost of everything and the value of nothing."

He looked as if I'd slapped him. "No, you're wrong, Maddie. I was only making conversation. I came here to apologize. For everything. That affair with Liz. It was stupid, wrong. A silly affair that got out of hand."

"For ten years? Ten years when I believed every word you told me. My God, you and Liz must have had a lot of laughs at my expense. Stupid, gullible Maddie who'll believe anything... I *loved* you, Neil. Have you any idea what that's really like? I truly loved you." Tears pricked my eyes. No, he mustn't see me cry. I forced them into retreat. "Now I don't believe I'll trust anyone ever again. That's one of the beauties of living here; I don't have to see anyone if I don't want to." *As long as I keep my door locked and don't answer the bell*, I didn't add.

Neil said nothing for a minute or two. He passed his hand over his face, inhaled deeply and leaned forward. "Is there really no way back for us, Maddie?"

Such arrogance! *"What?* Do you seriously believe for one moment that I'd take you back after all that's happened?"

"I realize now, I was stupid."

My mouth had gone dry. Every ounce of my will was focused on keeping my voice steady. "Yes. You were stupid. Very. But, contrary to what you may have thought then, *I'm* not. I was only stupid in one way. Loving and trusting *you*. Well, not anymore. I've put all that behind me. I assume this newfound awakening of yours has plenty to do with my inheritance? Of which, I may add, you are not entitled to one penny."

His face took on a pained expression. "Oh, Maddie, how could you think that? No, no of course it's nothing to do with your money. I want to come back to you. I still love you. I never really loved Liz. It was the excitement…" I could tell from his horrified expression that he knew he shouldn't have said that.

"Well you can go and find some other cheating woman to get your kicks with, because you're not coming here." I didn't know how much longer I could stop myself from letting fly at him. I stood up. "I think it's time you left."

I picked up his half-full coffee mug and empty brandy glass. "Time to go, Neil. I'd like to say it's been a pleasure, but it hasn't. Don't bother to come back."

He looked ashen. I could read his expression so clearly because I'd seen it before. He really had believed I would fall for his sob story and his phony contrition. His arrogance knew no bounds. How could I ever have doted on this man for so many years? Why had I never seen him for what he was—a money-obsessed womanizer?

I remained at the living room door. He must have seen I wouldn't back down, so he stood.

"Very well. I can see your mind's made up. I can't say how sorry I am. If you ever change your mind, I still have the same mobile number."

"*I* don't."

He nodded. "Can I first use your bathroom? It's an hour's drive back to Chester."

I pointed to the downstairs toilet and went into the kitchen.

I was rinsing his glass when I heard him shriek. I dropped it and it shattered in the sink.

Out in the hall, Neil was screaming and clutching his hair. If this was a new ruse, it was a pretty effective one.

I shook his arm. "What the hell are you playing at?"

His eyes were round, wide. "Something…there's something in that room…I saw it…I felt it…" He sank to his knees. "Oh, my God. What the hell was that?"

I pulled the toilet door wide open.

"*No*. Don't go in there, Maddie. *Please*."

I looked around at the tiny, white bathroom, with its toilet. Seat up, of course, as always when Neil was around. The faucets still ran in the small wash hand basin. I turned them off. They squeaked from lack of use. The overhead light illuminated my face in the mirror and the angry glint in my eyes. In a reflex action, I pushed a wayward lock of hair behind my ear and turned back into the hall.

"Nice try, but there's nothing here. Goodbye."

"I swear there was. On my life, Maddie, I swear I saw something."

"What did you see, Neil?"

"I don't know. I can't explain it. Like a…a…scarecrow. That's the nearest. Like a scarecrow. No eyes. Not a person. It touched me. It scratched me." He fingered his neck. "I can't feel anything now, but it hurt. You must be able to see. Look."

I ventured closer to him and peered at his throat. "All I can see are red marks where you've been rubbing it. There's no skin broken. Oh, come on, I've had enough of this. Time to go home."

I opened the front door and a cold breeze shot in, reminding me the nights were getting colder.

Neil lowered his hands, but they were shaking. For a moment I wondered if he was telling me the truth. Had he really seen something in there? I dismissed the thought. Another one of his pranks for getting his own way.

He took a few steps toward me. "Very well, I'll go. Something in this house—apart from you—doesn't want me here. Promise me you'll take care, Maddie. It might not want you here either."

"If you're trying to scare me, Neil, you're going to have to do an awful lot better than that."

"I'm not trying to scare you, Maddie. I know what I felt. I know what happened in there was real. There's something in this house. Something…not right. Promise me you'll be careful. Better still get the hell out of this place. You can afford it after all."

Any doubt in my mind flew away at that point. "Always money, Neil. Always money. Goodbye."

I practically shoved him out as I closed the door, locked and bolted it behind him.

In the downstairs bathroom, I put the seat down, switched off the light, and closed the door.

I made for the kitchen to clear up the mess and retrieve my glass. After that experience, I needed another drink. I switched on the light, stopped and stared.

The cellar door stood open. I knew it had been closed. I'd only been in a few minutes earlier and would have noticed it. I peered around the door and flicked the switch. With the extra lighting Charlie had fitted, the place wasn't nearly so dark and daunting. I still didn't feel like going down there though. Not when I was alone in the house.

"Hello." My voice echoed off the walls. Then silence. I listened for a few seconds. Nothing. I pulled the door shut. Just before it closed, I thought I heard a sound. As if someone was dragging something heavy across the floor. I shut the door with a bang and locked it.

I stood for a few moments, catching my breath, while my mind raced. Neil. I had to admit he had put the wind up me with his stories of something in the bathroom. There was a perfectly logical explanation for this. I had left the door open and, preoccupied with my unwelcome visitor, simply not noticed it earlier. The sound I had heard was probably the door dragging as I pulled it shut. Maybe it needed a bit of sanding down, although it had seemed to close easily enough.

The theory sounded good. If only it could have been true. Because, at three in the morning, when I still couldn't get to sleep, I remembered. Charlie had locked that door when he left. I'd seen him do it. And no one had opened it since.

Chapter Five

I lay there, listening to the stillness, alert for any slight sound, and jumped when the wind sent a shower rattling against the window.

Surely I had to be wrong. Neil couldn't have unlocked that door himself...or maybe I had missed him sneaking into the kitchen and opening it, to unnerve me. Try as I might, I couldn't see how he'd done it though. I had been with him the whole time, except when I went to the kitchen to make him coffee. And when he went to the bathroom, I followed him into the hall.

I fell asleep sometime in the early hours. When I awoke, the clock showed nine thirty. I yawned, stretched and the night's events flooded back. Strange, certainly, but somehow, with the sun shining once more, my fears had been pretty much washed away as if by the night's rain.

Today, I would busy myself by visiting the local shops and, unlike the previous occasions when I had bought what I needed and left with barely an exchange of words, I would make a concerted effort to talk to people. *If you don't feel confident, act as though you are.* I'd read that in a self-help book years earlier. It worked too, except that to do that, I needed to imagine myself as the adult version of the girl I had created for myself. Kelly. Unlike me, she would have grown up confident and self-assured. She would have had a career—maybe as a lawyer or doctor. As a child, I had always projected everything I wanted to be on to her. I hadn't called on her for years, but, with a little updating, she would carry me through.

Until I had grown in confidence enough to relax and be myself, Kelly would be the public face of Maddie—the one with the outgoing personality, able to strike up friendly conversations with total strangers.

I dressed carefully for my outing in navy blue boot-cut trousers, low-heeled black shoes, lightweight navy jacket, and white open-necked shirt. With my leather purse slung over my shoulder, I looked like a professional woman on my way to an important appointment. Kelly would approve, although she would have opted for a pencil skirt to emphasize her perfectly shaped legs. I tucked my hair behind my ears, took a deep breath, and opened the door.

I made my way up the steep hill of the High Street, aiming for the convenience store at the top. Along the way, I passed a row of small houses. Traffic thundered past me along a too-narrow thoroughfare. If ever a town needed a bypass it was this one. I passed the condemned block of apartments across the street. They looked innocuous enough. Bland, gray concrete, featureless windows, and a communal door, with half a dozen or so doorbells and postboxes on both sides. The day was overcast, but not cold, with a smell of autumnal damp leaves and wood fires in the air.

A black dog, similar to an unusually large Labrador—but with a fiercer expression—stood outside the apartments and glared at me. I shivered and hurried on.

A few people passed me. One or two said, "Good morning," and I returned their greetings. I hadn't a clue who they were. They were being neighborly and I liked that. Soon, all being well, I would know all their names and be able to greet them properly, inquire after their various offspring, siblings, parents, and any related events or ailments. Soon, I would be part of this community. And Kelly was going to help me get there.

I picked up milk, a newspaper I probably wouldn't read, a bar of chocolate, and made for the counter. I took a deep breath and imagined Kelly standing there in my place, poised and confident.

"Hello, I'm Maddie Chambers. I've moved into Hargest House." I extended my hand over a selection of impulse buys—candy bars of all kinds, chewing gum, licorice.

The assistant smiled and nodded. "Thought you might be. You fit the description. I'm June Hughes. I own this shop. My nephew Charlie's doing some work for you."

I shook her hand and also smiled. "News travels fast."

"You'll get used to that here. And the fact everyone pretty much knows everyone else's business. They're probably related to them too."

"It's a small town. I'm afraid I'm more used to the city, although I did spend summers here as a child."

The smile faded. "With old Miss Grant. She was your aunt, I believe?"

"Yes. Did you know her?"

June handed me my purchases. "Not very well. I don't think most people did, towards the end. She never went out, you see. Had people to 'do' for her."

June didn't sound as if she approved of people having others to 'do' for them. Or maybe something else was on her mind. Her tone had become almost frosty.

"Well, it's been nice to meet you. I'm sure I'll be in again soon."

June's smile ended at the corners of her lips. "Yes, do. I'll look forward to it." The words and the expression didn't match. And I knew which I believed.

I had been putting off sorting out Aunt Charlotte's bedroom, but a nagging thought that maybe—just maybe—I might find some answers, hardened my resolve to go in there. I opened the door to the scent of lavender. A massive bowl, crammed to the hilt with dried blooms, stood on top of a chest of drawers. Under the large bay window stood a desk, covered in photos. Here is where I would start. I set down the large empty cardboard box I had brought with me and sat on the stool. The desk was a traditional, light oak with a polished top, a blotter, and a pen holder—containing an eclectic mix of Parker fountain pens, propelling pencils, and cheap ballpoints.

One by one, I picked up the photos in their silver frames. There were two taken of me. One on my own, holding a kitten I couldn't remember—but definitely not mine. Mother wouldn't allow animals in the house and Aunt Charlotte never had any, as far as I could remember. The other photograph of me was with my aunt. She was holding my hand and I was smiling. Aunt Charlotte's expression bothered me. She was standing at a slight angle, looking over my head, as if something had caught her attention that concerned her.

The other photos were of the rear garden I had barely explored since I returned. Here it was, as I remembered it from my childhood, in full rosy magnificence—complete with the beautiful, aromatic lavender border whose bounty now fragranced her room.

I took hold of the brass handles and pulled open the top drawer. Inside, notepaper and envelopes were neatly arranged on one side, while on the other, I found a book—leather bound, with a gold-colored clasp. My heart beat a little faster as I lifted it out, and I hesitated before snapping it open. A pang of conscience hit me. I may be about to intrude on my aunt's most intimate secrets. I nearly put it back, but my desperate need for answers made me flip it open. It was a notebook which I quickly discovered—as I flipped through the pages—Aunt Charlotte had adapted into an occasional diary. A page-long entry would be followed by a gap of days, or weeks, until the next one. Most of the earlier entries concerned her gardening or the shortcomings of some of the staff she had employed on Nathaniel's behalf. One entry was dated June 16th, 1960.

I played "Serenade in Blue" for Mr. Hargest on the piano today. If ever the old saying about music soothing the savage breast was true, it is true of his reaction to it. He had been reading in the library and startled me when he opened the door. I thought he was going to tell me to stop, and be quite angry for disturbing him, but on the contrary.

"What is that song, Charlotte?" he asked. He put his hands on the piano, and I noticed his palms were flat on the surface, not clenched or in any way threatening.

"It's an old Glenn Miller song," I told him. "I've always loved his music but I think 'Serenade in Blue' is my favorite. It brings back memories." I didn't tell him they were bittersweet and that for ten years or more I couldn't bear to hear it or play it. Now, I seem to want to do both all the time. Perhaps that is a signal I have moved on.

"I have never heard it before," he said and I must have looked startled, because he laughed—the first time I can ever remember him laugh. "I never listen to popular music," he said. "Only classical. But henceforward, 'Serenade in Blue' will also be my favorite. You can play it as often as you wish."

He couldn't have surprised me more. I wish he hadn't spoiled it by looking at me in that way that makes me so uncomfortable. His eyes seem to pierce through to my soul, as if he is trying to possess me. Sometimes I think I shall have to leave this place and find another position but where would I go? It isn't easy being a woman alone in this world. Especially one without any money or much family to support her.

Oh, Aunt Charlotte, I thought. Surely, even in 1960, you didn't have to stay where you felt uneasy around your boss. But that was over fifty years ago, I reminded myself. A different world—especially for women.

I read on, discovering things about my aunt's life she had never talked about. To me, at any rate.

Playing "our" song reminded me of that wonderful summer with Freddie before he turned 18 and joined up. 1944. How long ago it seems and yet, in another way, it could have been yesterday. We went to the village midsummer dance and I wore a blue dress I'd made from an old gown of Mother's she no longer wore. I was so proud of myself for saving on my coupons.

"You look a proper sight for sore eyes," Freddie said as he led me out onto the dance floor. The band struck up a familiar Glenn Miller song. Freddie held me close and hummed along with the melody. "You'll always be my 'Serenade in Blue'," he said.

I was so happy, tears filled my eyes. Some must have spilled over onto Freddie's cheek because he stopped dancing.

"What's the matter? Did I say something wrong?" He looked so worried, poor lamb.

"Oh no," I said, feeling silly. "You said everything perfectly. As always."

He smiled and I loved the way his eyes creased up. Such a handsome man, my Freddie.

"You're my girl now, Lottie," he said. No one ever called me Lottie but him. Always Charlotte. Not Freddie. I was always his Lottie. "Promise me you'll wait for me. And that you'll write to me every day I'm away."

"I promise, Freddie. Come home safely."

"I will. Jerry won't catch me. You'll see. I'll be strolling up your path again in no time."

But you never did, did you, Freddie? Six months later your plane was shot down over the North Sea and I thought my world had ended. Part of it had.

Today, all I have are the memories. No one—not even Nathaniel Hargest—can take those away from me. And now I can bear to listen to "our" song and play it again. I have my employer's blessing to do so any time I choose. Who would have guessed it? Perhaps Mr. Hargest does have a heart after all.

A tear splashed onto the page and I wiped my eyes with the back of my hand. In all those years, I'd had no idea Aunt Charlotte hugged these secret memories to herself. I wondered if Mother ever knew about Freddie.

I sighed and turned the pages. Occasionally my aunt made mention of her employer's uncertain temper. An entry for November 30th, 1960 read:

Mr. Hargest ordered me to fire the cook today. For the second time in a week she overcooked the cabbage. It was lucky I had my wits about me when he summoned me to tell me. He had a heavy glass paperweight in his hand which sailed close past me and smashed against the wall. His anger is something to be avoided at all costs. Needless to say I sent the cook packing! Goodness alone knows where I'll find another one. News travels fast in this town and even as far as Rokesby Green. There's nothing for it. I shall have to advertise in The Lady. *I'm afraid Mr. Hargest won't like the cost, but what am I to do?*

I read on, past 1960 and into 1961, right up until May 1964 where, curiously, some pages had been ripped out. Those that remained contained little enlightening information. Most entries concerned my aunt's increasing discomfort with Nathaniel Hargest's behavior although, infuriatingly, she revealed little in the way of detail beyond the occasional mention of her employer's temper tantrums.

Then there was a gap until 1967 and an entry for June 1st:

I have taken up gardening. I find it comforting and quite therapeutic. I am hopeful of an excellent first bean harvest. My little vegetable garden has given me something to concentrate on. It has helped reduce the pain of the last couple of years and, of course, the kitchen benefits. Not that Mr. Hargest notices.

News of little Madeleine's birth has given me renewed hope. Maybe, in spite of everything, what they have told me is true. Maybe all will be well after all.

There the makeshift diary ended, with nearly half its pages blank. I was more perplexed than ever. Who had told her all would be well? I hadn't a clue what that was about. I was beginning to think I hadn't really known Aunt Charlotte at all. She had harbored so many secrets. My sense of unease cranked up a notch.

I put the book back where I had found it.

The second drawer initially revealed nothing except a slim, black book, bound in leather. I picked it up and opened it. *Book of Shadows* was embossed in gold on the front. I remembered reading about those once. Wiccans had them. They wrote spells inside them, or favorite sayings, words of wisdom, potions and so on. Turning the pages revealed that Aunt Charlotte had filled hers with poems and recipes, but one curious little entry caught my attention. Headed, simply, "Willow", it listed a number of occult uses of the tree—from carving talismans, to rituals for protection and for summoning spirits.

Spirits of willow protect me. Spirits of willow come to me. Spirits of willow let no harm come from the darkness and the evil ones…

May the Lord and his Lady protect me through this holy willow…

I put the book down and rummaged through the drawer. My fingers closed on something and I pulled it out. A slim, tapering twig had been fashioned into a wand. A further dig and I pulled out a small wooden pendant on a broken necklace of thin leather. The delicate carving was of the pagan figure known as the Green Man. I stared at it in wonder. I couldn't remember Aunt Charlotte ever mentioning anything to do with the occult and yet here she was with books of spells, magical rituals and, as for the lavender I had thought so innocently pretty, it turned out that too had magical connotations.

I went back to the Book of Shadows and flipped through more pages of spells, folklore of the willow and potions. On the last page, I read an entry different than all the others. It was undated:

Now he tells me I must share his bed. He has ordered me to dismiss all the other servants. We are to manage with whoever the temp agency sends us and I am to do the rest. Mr. Hargest doesn't want any more prying eyes and wagging tongues, although how he will prevent them I haven't a clue. It doesn't matter to him that I am so much younger than he is and the sight of his ancient body revolts me. I will have to lie there in the dark and bear it. May the Lord and his Lady protect me.

I flipped to the next page and the next after that, but those that weren't ripped out were all blank. Like the diary. I wondered when she had written that sad, resigned entry, but had no way of knowing, unless I could find anything else that might give me a hint. I left the *Book of Shadows* on top of the desk and pulled the drawers out fully. I peered underneath, hoping I might find a secret drawer, or something wedged. Nothing.

For the rest of the afternoon, I went through Aunt Charlotte's wardrobe, reaching into pockets, folding her coats, dresses, skirts, and tops and placing them gently in the box. I would take them to the nearest charity shop the following day.

I emptied every drawer of the chest under the bowl of lavender, but all I found were neatly folded underclothes and woolens. I even stripped the bed of its heavy, embroidered coverlet and lifted the mattress. Nothing.

Eventually, I had to admit defeat. But only after I had taken down every picture and examined the frame for any hidden document. No, whatever my aunt knew about Nathaniel Hargest, or this house, she had taken with her to her grave. I hesitated before returning the *Book of Shadows* to the drawer, but at least I would know where it was should I need it. There was something spooky about such a thing and

I was reluctant to have it in close proximity to me, however paranoid that might sound.

"I can't go up there, Mrs. Chambers." Pete Evans shook his head with such vigor his baseball cap wobbled.

"Whyever not, Pete?" Charlie's brother had been perfectly happy to come straight over when I asked him to do some more decorating for me. Now, as soon as I mentioned the second floor, his face paled.

"I'd rather you not ask me about that. I can't. I'm really sorry, but no. I'll willingly do down here for you." He looked around at the walls of the kitchen where we were standing. "I'll do the next floor, but I'm not going up any further than that."

"Do you have a problem with heights or something?"

"No. No. Nothing like that. I'm the first one up a ladder any day of the week. I just…I'd rather not talk about it. Is there anything else I can do for you today?" He inched his way to the door.

"No, not that I can think of at the moment." I was still trying to work out what his problem was. "Are you sure you won't change your mind? I don't understand what is so wrong with that floor."

Pete hesitated. "Look, I'm sure if you asked someone from outside the town, they'd probably come and do the job in a flash. Don't ask anyone from around here though. Not if you don't want another rejection."

So it was all down to local gossip. A coil of annoyance spiraled up my body. Temptation to make some sarcastic remark almost overwhelmed me, but what good would it have done? Pete's mind was made up and closed. End of subject. I would have to find someone else or leave it in its current, shabby state when I had hoped to brighten it up for the theater group.

After he'd gone, I decided to ring the only person I knew who might be sympathetic. Shona.

She laughed when I told her Pete's reaction. "Oh, I can tell you what that was about. The local tabbies have the story that Mr. Hargest and your aunt's satanic rituals took place either at the tree or in one of the rooms on that floor. The top floor was allegedly used for sacrifices. Not human ones. Chickens mainly. Although there were some rumors during Mr. Hargest's time, but that was just people's weird imaginations again. Someone goes missing and straightaway it has to be down to the most unpopular person in town. He was never charged with anything, and nether was she."

"*What?* Seriously? They really believe this stuff?"

"Oh yes. Very superstitious lot around here."

"Have you told the Am Dram Group that they'll be rehearsing up there?"

"I've mentioned it. One or two hesitated a bit, but I think they believe they've got safety in numbers, and a couple of them are relatively new to the area anyway and won't have any truck with such stuff."

"The thing is, my Aunt Charlotte was such a kind, gentle person. She was very free and easy about my comings and goings and great fun to be with. If I'm honest, far more than my own mother, who always seemed to be wrapped up in her work, my father and their safaris to really notice what I was doing." I realized I was revealing far more about myself than I ever did. And to someone I hardly knew. Over the phone! "Anyway, suffice it to say that the Aunt Charlotte I knew was hardly the type to indulge in devil worship."

There was a pause on the other end of the line.

"Shona? Are you still there?"

"Yes, I'm here. Sorry. Look, you didn't see your aunt for many years, Maddie. People change, you know. Maybe she got involved with an occult group of some kind. A cult perhaps."

I thought for a moment. "Well, anything's possible, I suppose." Into my mind flashed image after image of Aunt Charlotte laughing, smiling, running her fingers through her ash blonde hair which may, or may not, have owed something to a hairdresser's coloring skills. I pictured her embroidering tablecloths, or reading. Nevil Shute was her favorite author. Then there was her music. That old gramophone upstairs and her piano. She would play a little Chopin, or more modern tunes. She could read music, but could also play by ear and thought nothing of attempting some song that was riding high in the charts at the time. I remembered singing "Ebony and Ivory" with her and Dexy's Midnight Runners' "Come on Eileen". Song after song. She only had to hear it a couple of times before she could play it. Sometimes we'd sing some of the songs from her youth. But she always came back to her favorite—"Serenade in Blue"—and when she did, a wistful look used to come into her eyes. Now, of course, I knew why. Freddie. An image of the dusty record on the turntable shot into my mind and a shiver coursed through my veins. I had no idea why I should repeatedly have such a reaction to a song I had learned had held such romantic significance for my aunt.

"I can't see it, Shona. I cannot equate Aunt Charlotte with some madwoman slicing the heads off chickens and prancing around nude in the garden. It doesn't make sense."

Shona sighed. "I'm sure you're right and it's all a lot of nonsense. Anyway, we'll look forward to our first rehearsal next Monday."

I rang off soon after. I wandered out into the hall and looked upward, to the landing at the top of the staircase. I heard a noise and caught my breath. A child's laughter. The sound of running feet.

Terrified, I gripped the banister and crept up the stairs. The farther I climbed, the louder the laughter. I reached the first floor and heard it again. It came from above.

I felt as if I'd slipped into a dream. My feet moved automatically, one step after the other, following the sound, up to the second floor.

As soon as my foot touched the top step, the laughter stopped. My heart thumped, but I had to go on. I had to see where that sound had come from.

All the doors were closed. The landing felt quite warm; the new radiator was doing a great job. Gone was the fusty, unaired smell.

I turned the handle of the first door I came to. It opened. Inside struck cold. This was the largest room, the one that would be perfect for rehearsals. There was no furniture except a free-standing tall cupboard at the far end. I knew from my earlier investigations this was empty, apart from a handful of dead woodlice on the bottom. I'd have to clean those out too.

The walls were drab, with faded wallpaper coming unstuck in places. The bare windows were tall, wide. I peered out. They afforded a perfect view for anyone looking up from the riverside walk. At night, with the lights on, onlookers would be able to see anyone standing by the window, as I now was. Did they look up and see Aunt Charlotte doing something a little odd? Did someone's warped imagination turn it into a sinister act, embellish it and sully her reputation for evermore? I would probably never know.

I drifted so far into my own thoughts, I almost forgot what had brought me up there in the first place.

A child's laugh rang out. Whoever it was had joined me in the same room. I spun around. Out of the corner of my eye I caught a glimpse of a young girl in a yellow dress, short white ankle socks, and plaited blonde hair, running out of the door. I dashed out into the corridor. No one there. I looked down the stairs. No one. I hurried along, opening doors. All empty.

A childish giggle sounded from the first room. I raced back, in time to see the doors of the cupboard swing slowly shut. Without thinking, I dashed over and wrenched them open.

The cupboard was empty.

I let out a cry, charged down the stairs and into the living room, aiming straight for the brandy bottle, but I trembled so much I could barely pour and kept spilling it onto the table. I must calm down. I emptied my glass in one gulp and refilled it, coughing as the harsh liquid burned my throat.

That child. The child that couldn't be there. But she was, wasn't she? Impossible as it may seem. I recognized her. I knew the little girl with the blonde plaits and the yellow cotton dress. I knew her because I had created her. Veronica. The youngest of my imaginary siblings. And she was here, in this house.

From far away, the strains of "Serenade in Blue" invaded my mind. I told myself I was imagining it. If only that were true.

Chapter Six

I awoke to the doorbell ringing. My stiffened limbs objected to my feeble efforts to stretch them, and my attempt to raise my throbbing head off the cushion was thwarted by a thundering, clamorous roar of pain. I sank back down again. Thor had acquired an extra set of hammers and had decided to test them out on my brain. Through the murky mush of my mind, memories of last night drifted back. I'd drunk far too much brandy and fallen asleep—or unconscious—on the settee.

The doorbell rang again, sending fresh agonies surging through my head. I tried to sit up. Failed. No way could I get to the door in this state, besides I could taste bile in my mouth. My first destination had to be the downstairs bathroom.

I just made it.

The doorbell fell silent. Whoever it was had given up.

I struggled into the kitchen, the world swimming before my eyes. I clung on to anything within reach—the wall, the fitted units—and inched my way to the sink. I grabbed a glass from the draining board, filled it with cold water from the faucet and gulped it down. I splashed clear, cold water over my face, soaking my hair in the process. My head still banged but at least I felt a little more conscious. I rummaged in a drawer, found a box of Panadol and downed two with three more glasses of water.

Black coffee. With sugar. Lots of it. I sat, nursing my steaming mug, my eyes closed. Too ill to be scared. Self-inflicted wounds, not worthy of sympathy, not even my own.

An hour later, the coffee and pills had done their job and I was feeling well enough to think about what I'd heard and seen. Or rather, what I thought I'd heard and seen. Because I couldn't really have seen her, could I? My mind must be playing tricks on me.

For the next day or two, I didn't venture beyond the first floor, but when the following Monday arrived, I had no choice. I'd promised Shona I would heat their room up. The cast was due to arrive for a seven thirty start that same evening. Contrary to my earlier resolve, I hadn't baked a cake. Maybe Wednesday, in time for their next rehearsal.

The brand new convector heaters stood in the hall. My stomach lurched at the thought of going into that room again, but the sun was shining on a beautiful autumnal day. Outside, blue sky, white clouds. Everything normal. Nothing out of place. If I kept telling myself that, I'd be fine. Just fine.

I picked up one of the heaters. It weighed little, but the awkward shape meant I could only carry one at a time. I took a deep breath and climbed up to the second floor. This time I heard no childish laughter or running footsteps, only my own.

I set the heater down at one end of the room, plugged it in and switched it on. Almost immediately an acrid stench of burning hit my nose. The smell of a new heater, but unpleasant. I really should have tried them out earlier. Too late. I would have to apologize and spray a bit of air freshener around.

I placed the second heater at the opposite side of the room and the burning aromas met in the middle. Maybe the smell would wear off by the time they turned up. I could live in hope.

At seven fifteen, they began to arrive. A friendly bunch trying hard to pretend they weren't curious about the house they had heard so much about, and its new owner. One by one, I showed them upstairs. Now there were other people here, I no longer felt afraid. The more chatter and laughter I heard, the more my earlier fears melted away.

Shona rang the doorbell at seven thirty. She looked flushed. "I'm not late, am I? I hate being late, but I got a phone call at the last minute. I bet they're all here, aren't they?"

I took her coat. "If you were expecting fourteen, they are. I'll show you up."

"Oh no, Maddie, there's no need, I'll follow the noise!"

An hour later, I took them tea and biscuits. The rehearsal seemed to be going well and the group seemed to have made themselves at home.

"I realize I didn't tell you where the bathroom is on this floor," I said, handing them drinks.

"Oh, no need," said a woman who looked around thirty, with bright red hair. She had introduced herself as Cynthia. "The young girl showed me."

I stared. My mouth dropped open. My hand trembled and I spilled coffee. A few faces peered at me, concerned.

Shona touched my arm "Are you all right, Maddie? You're awfully pale."

I ignored her. "What did this girl look like? Little, with blonde plaits? Yellow dress?"

Cynthia shook her head, sending her ringlet-like curls bouncing. "No. She was around twelve or thirteen, I think. Short light brown hair, in a bob—rather like yours actually."

I touched my hair. My heart thumped. The entire cast had stopped talking, all eyes fixed on my exchange with Cynthia. Shona frowned.

I licked my dry lips. "Can you describe what she was wearing?"

Cynthia raised her eyes, as if searching heaven for the answer. "I didn't really take too much notice, I'm afraid. I assumed she was your daughter or someone. I think she had a blue dress on, with a full skirt."

Her words came to me through a fog. I had to find out the rest. "Was it 1970s style? Did she have clunky platform sandals?" I knew what her answer would be.

"Yes that's it. I didn't like to say old-fashioned. Some people can get quite offended if you…" Her voice tailed away as she took in my expression.

Shona put her arm around me. "Who is she, Maddie? Do you have a guest staying here?"

I shook my head. "I'm sorry. I'm interrupting your rehearsal."

I half ran out of the room and charged down the stairs. Shona found me in the living room, shaking and unscrewing the top of the brandy bottle. She gently removed it from my hand.

"That isn't going to solve anything. You know that. Why don't you tell me what happened? Who was the girl who showed Cynthia the bathroom?"

Tears flowed freely down my cheeks. How could I explain something I didn't even understand myself?

"That girl. She doesn't exist. Except in my mind."

Shona blinked rapidly. "I'm sorry, I don't understand. Cynthia saw her."

"And that's what *I* don't understand." I swiped at the tears with the back of my hand. "You know lots of kids invent imaginary friends? Well, years ago, when I came here as a child, I had an imaginary brother and three sisters. Last week, I was sure I caught sight of the youngest of them. Veronica. Now Cynthia has seen another imaginary sister of mine. Sonia." Even as I spoke the words I realized how ridiculous they sounded.

Shona sat abruptly, as if someone had shoved her. She looked down at her hands in her lap. Right now I could tell she hadn't a clue what to say. Neither did I. I inwardly prayed she wouldn't tell the others, who must already have decided that Charlotte Grant's niece was every bit as flaky as they thought *she* had been.

"Shona. I don't know what to do. I must sound crazy. But Cynthia described her exactly as I created her. And there's no one else in this house apart from the fifteen of you, and me. So, if she isn't who I say she is, who else can it be?"

Shona shook her head and looked up at me, her eyes troubled. "At this moment, I haven't a clue. I could say intruders, but a burglar hardly dresses in platform sandals and directs you to the bathroom."

"I chased after the child I saw, but she disappeared. I dare say we could hunt high and low, all over the house for this latest one, and we'd never find her. Because she doesn't exist."

Shona stood. She looked awkward. "I'm so sorry, I must get back to the rehearsal. They'll wonder where I've got to. Shall I come and see you tomorrow? We can have a chat about this and try to get to the bottom of it."

"I don't know if I'll be here tomorrow."

Shona's eyes widened. "Well if you're going to drive anywhere, don't touch that stuff." She nodded toward the brandy.

"No, I wouldn't. I don't believe in drinking and driving."

"Good. I'm so sorry I can't invite you to stay at my house, or I would."

She didn't elaborate. Probably didn't have enough space, I thought. I realized I didn't know much about Shona's personal life or any job she might have. She must have far more information about me than I did about her. "I'll be fine, honestly," I said. "I think I will get out of this house tonight though. I'll go down to the Premier Inn down the road. Maybe things will seem a bit clearer in the morning. I'll go and pack a bag and be ready to leave when you finish your rehearsal. Would you do me a favor and stay with me until I'm ready to go?"

Shona hugged me. "Of course. And don't worry, I'm sure we'll solve this little puzzle. There's bound to be a rational explanation."

"I wish I knew what it was."

When I snapped the light on in the kitchen, I saw the coffee mugs ready to be washed. Someone had brought the tray down. At least I wouldn't have to go back up there tonight. As long as one of the cast thought to switch the heaters off.

As I washed and dried the crockery, I kept going over and over it all in my mind. If Cynthia had seen Sonia, maybe I really had seen Veronica. But as to why—and, more significantly, how—we could have seen two figments of my imagination, I had no idea.

I emptied the bowl and the water gurgled down the drain and through the pipes. For some reason, the thought of the tree roots in my cellar came into my mind. That again was something that simply shouldn't exist. Not like that, at any rate.

The kitchen door closed behind me with a sharp click. I caught my breath. It had been wide open. It didn't normally close by itself. Someone had closed it.

I tugged at the handle. It opened. No one in the hall. I peered up the stairs. No one there either. I raced over into the living room. Empty. I smelled perfume. The distinctive scent of Opium—my imaginary sister Thelma's favorite scent.

Then it started. Faint, as if coming from far away. Glenn Miller and His Orchestra. My aunt's distinctive voice, singing along to the record. "…'Serenade in Blue'…"

Something stirred inside me. A sharp click in my brain, like the kitchen door closing. I sank to my knees.

"What do you want? Who are you? Why are you doing this?" I sounded like a frightened little girl, my voice no more than a whimper.

A whiff of cigarette smoke prickled my nostrils, as if someone were smoking nearby. I glanced over my shoulder, terrified I would see who was responsible for it. Praying that if I did, it would be one of the cast.

No one there. No one in the room at all, except me and the faintest trail of pungent smoke. In the distance, the song faded into silence.

Tom. He smoked. Thelma and Sonia were always on at him to quit, but he said that made him want to smoke more. When Thelma caught me—the Kelly me—sneaking a quick drag, she really laid into him. I remembered that from when I was about ten.

I shook my head. It must be me. Somehow I was doing something to make these imaginary characters real. Had I developed some weird type of brain disease that caused imaginary creations from my childhood to manifest themselves in the real world?

Or was it this house?

My mind raced. There could be only one decision. Put Hargest House on the market. Sell it. Use the money to buy somewhere much newer. Something small and far away from here. There was something about this town too. The jinxed apartment block on the

High Street. That mysterious fire that drove the vicar to early retirement. The dog.

And the willow—the tentacle tree—defying nature and growing roots more than fifty yards long, somehow meshing with this house.

I had to ask the question, what had Aunt Charlotte been up to here? Was it only idle gossip from people jealous of her good fortune in inheriting such wealth? Or was there something far more sinister? Were memories locked in the walls of this building? Had my return somehow released them? Questions, always questions. Never answers.

I ran up to my bedroom, took a small suitcase down from the top of the wardrobe and threw in clothes, underwear and toiletries. I grabbed my purse and sat down on the bed.

Above me, the rehearsal was in full swing. I checked my watch. Nine fifteen. Shona said they usually packed in at around nine thirty. Of course, I would have to return here on Wednesday to open up and heat the room. I couldn't bear to think of it. I could give the keys to Shona. They could let themselves in, have the run of the place. I didn't care. As long as I didn't have to be here.

But I couldn't do that, could I? Shona knew I was scared. For all I knew, she could be too. Maybe the whole cast was. Maybe they'd tell me they didn't want to come here anymore because of the weird things that were happening. I could shut up the house and hand everything over to an estate agent.

The jumble of thoughts tumbled over one another in my mind. I grabbed my bags and, with a sob, made my way back down to the living room.

Shortly after nine thirty, Shona came in. Through the open door, voices came closer, down the stairs. The rehearsal had finished for the night.

Shona looked more relaxed than an hour ago. "Thank you for letting us use that room, Maddie. It's perfect for our rehearsals. I do hope you'll let us carry on. It's so hard to find affordable rehearsal space around here. We did wonder at one time if we would have to disband, but you came to our rescue. So we'll see you again on Wednesday. Is that all right with you?"

I wanted to say, "No," but couldn't. She was being so kind. They could continue to use the house over the weeks and months it would take to find a buyer. It was even less salable now, with a tree growing in the cellar, and God alone knew what else going on.

"I see you've packed a fair bit of luggage." Shona's frown returned. "Would you rather we didn't come back?"

"Oh no, no, that will be fine." What on earth was "fine" about my situation, I hadn't a clue. "I'll see you all on Wednesday."

The frown vanished, replaced with a broad smile. "That's great. I switched the heaters off up there, and the lights, so you just need to lock up. I'll come out with you."

Cynthia and another cast member were enjoying a cigarette outside. I opened the door in time to hear her say, "…flaky, like her aunt."

Our eyes met. At least she had the grace to look embarrassed. She gave me a nervous, twitchy smile, cast her eyes downward, and moved off with her friend. I heard giggles when they must have thought they were out of earshot.

Great. No doubt the whole town would have decided I was a head case by lunchtime the next day. If I hadn't already decided to leave, that would have done it. I could go wherever I pleased. And at this moment, that meant anywhere but here.

Chapter Seven

Two days away from the house and already I was putting things into perspective. Not only that, my desperate quest for answers had quashed some of my apprehensions. Of course, leaning on Kelly helped too. She would view the facts rationally. Anything irrational was simply a mystery waiting to be solved. Maybe my self-therapy would seem crazy to most people, but it worked for me, and at this moment, that was all that mattered. Anything to help me get through this with some semblance of sanity remaining.

On Wednesday morning, rain beat on the windows of my hotel room on the first really bad day of the new season.

I stared out at the dripping landscape. Gray, sodden. As I ventured outside, a chill wind whipped my cheeks, making them smart. I pulled the zip of my shower jacket up to my chin and secured the hood. No point attempting an umbrella in this weather. Fallen leaves created a treacherous mush underfoot. I unlocked my car and hesitated. So far, I'd paid for three nights and this would be my last. Should I extend my stay? I was comfortable enough. I slept well, felt safe. I could have paid a lot more for luxury in Chester, but here I was near enough to home to be able to carry on pretty much as normal. Maybe I would see the estate agent today. It all depended on what happened when I got back to Hargest House.

The rain had stopped when I climbed out of my car and stared up at the Gothic towers of Nathaniel Hargest's pride and joy. I was glad we'd never met. I would have hated his arrogance, cruelty, and selfish ego. Had he built all that into this house?

I shivered. The air held a distinct chill and the damp penetrated my clothes and seeped into my body. I smelled the autumn aromas of rotting vegetation, leaf mold and sodden wood. I sniffed. Someone somewhere had lit a log fire. That, at least, provided a homely, comforting smell. For a second, a memory flashed through my mind, too fleeting to hold. A blazing log fire, the distinctive aroma of burning applewood, reminding me of those colder nights at Aunt Charlotte's. We had never had real fires at home. Mother said it made too much mess. I shivered at the memory of ice-cold mornings, the condensation freezing the curtains to the windowsills. I'd drag my school clothes into bed and get dressed under the covers before emerging and summoning up courage to brave the bathroom and the water out of the hot tap that never seemed to struggle above lukewarm.

A sudden wave of embarrassment surged inside me. I had made such a fool of myself on Monday, I worried how the cast would react to me this evening. I hadn't even been into any of the local shops since, so had no way of knowing if I had become the main topic of conversation. But I suspected so. I had provided too good a morsel to resist.

I opened the front door and stepped inside, looking all around me as I did so, fearful of what I might see. The hall felt warm, but I would need to turn up the heating, with the colder weather on its way—even if I was selling the place. Potential buyers liked to be wooed by warmth, coziness, comfort. I wandered into the living room and then the kitchen. I set my purse down on the worktop, removed my sodden jacket and draped it around a chair.

The only sound was the ticking of various clocks in each room. I noticed the cellar door—firmly shut—and breathed a sigh of relief.

I toyed with the idea of making myself a coffee, but decided I'd do it after I'd switched those heaters on. If I decided to stay here for the rest of the day.

I left the kitchen and started up the stairs. My heart beat a little faster but, when I got there, the only sound on the second floor was me. *My* breathing. *My* footsteps. *My* hand turning the door handle, making it squeak and the door creak as I opened it. Inside, a few theatrical props lay around. They'd set up a small table, with a lamp. A few chairs were scattered about. I recognized some of them from the room that had been used as a general dumping ground. So they'd made themselves at home all right, even to the extent of exploring other rooms. I didn't mind. That must have been when that woman had bumped into Sonia…

I stopped myself. She couldn't have seen Sonia, I reminded myself. Sonia didn't exist. Except in my mind where she had lain, ignored, for over thirty-five years.

The heaters began to take the damp chill off the room within minutes. Glancing out of the window, I saw a couple walking with their Golden Labrador down the river path. They didn't see me; they were moving in the opposite direction. The woman stooped and unclipped the leash from the dog's collar. Freed from his restraint, he bounded along ahead of them, full of life and enthusiasm as young dogs are. I watched him gallop off toward the tentacle tree. He stopped, cocked his leg, and overbalanced. Shocked, I watched him lying still, on the ground.

The couple raced over to him. The woman gesticulated wildly. The man grabbed his phone from his jacket pocket. The dog lifted his head, as if he had recovered from being stunned. The couple helped him to his feet and he shook himself. The man put away his phone as the woman replaced the leash. The Labrador barked and strained, pulling her away from the willow. If the couple looked up now, they would see me staring down at them. I backed away. What had happened to make that dog react like that? What was it about that tree?

I scanned the room again, relieved to see everything looked normal.

The doorbell rang, faint and distant up here. I closed the door behind me and hurried down the stairs. A gray-haired man in a high visibility yellow jacket stood on my doorstep. He held a clipboard in his dirty hands.

"Mrs. Chambers?"

"Yes?"

"I'm Terry Watson from Priory Tree Services. You called us about a problem in your cellar."

I had completely forgotten. "I'm sorry, did we say today?"

"Not definitely. I said I'd call next time I was doing a job in the area. I'm on my way there, so I thought I'd see if I could catch you. Is it convenient, or would you prefer me to call back?"

"Oh no, no, now is fine." He'd caught me unawares but, after all, whatever I decided to do with the house, those tree roots had to go. One way or another. "I'll show you. It's through here. Would you like a cup of tea or coffee?"

"Oh no, thanks, I'm fine."

I opened the cellar door and switched on the light.

"At least I won't need my torch," he said. "Some cellars are like the black hole of Calcutta." He started down the stairs, his boots clattering on the wooden steps.

I called after him. "This one was pretty dark until a week or so ago."

He reached the bottom, turned around and grinned at me. I lost sight of him as he went to investigate. I heard scuffling and he spoke.

"Ah, here it is." More scuffling and a dragging noise. I stayed at the top of the stairs and waited. Seconds ticked by. Nothing. The hairs rose on the back of my neck.

"Are you all right down there?"

He moved back into the light at the bottom of the stairs. The smile had been replaced by a frown.

"You told me on the phone that you thought it was a willow? Well, that's the weirdest willow tree I've ever seen," he said. "They're not usually too invasive. It's the type of tree that takes no for an answer. You know, if you put up some sort of barrier—anything from pool lining to foundations—they stop growing there. Their roots also tend to be much closer to the surface. They need water, and the roots extract that from soil, so they're usually found within a foot or so of the surface. Only in dry, sandy conditions will they have to grow deeper. The soil round here is neither sandy nor dry. You're right by the river, so the roots should be really close to the surface. In this case, this tree isn't pushing up under your foundations; it's like it's part of them. I don't get it at all. I'm not even sure what to do about it really. I mean, we could cut off the roots, but… I can't believe I'm saying this. From what I've seen, if we do, it might affect the integrity of your foundation."

He started up the stairs and I backed away to let him pass while I tried to take in what he'd said. "So you're saying that when this house was built, the tree roots were put in as part of the foundation?"

"Not put in, exactly. Look, I don't really know what I'm saying because what I've seen is impossible. It's as if the tree somehow mixed in with the foundations and supported them. But that's not how it's supposed to work. Not at all. If anything, trees are supposed to destabilize foundations by pushing against them. This one has become part of them. Basically, your house is built on a foundation comprised of the usual hardcore, bricks, mortar—and an enormous tree root." He opened the kitchen door, to go outside. "I have some tools in the van, I'll dig some small trenches outside to try and trace the source. The actual tree. That's confusing me as well, because the nearest seems to be that one down by the river, but it's too far away. Much too far away. Maybe these roots belong to a tree that was felled. I'll go and investigate."

"Don't you have another job you have to get to?"

"That'll have to wait an hour or so. I'll give the customer a call and tell her I've been held up."

I made a coffee and sat in my kitchen. The cellar door stood open. A cool, damp breeze wafted up, bringing with it the now-familiar woody, damp earth smell.

Curiosity took hold of me. I had to go back down there and see what the arborist had seen. Impossible surely, but hadn't Charlie reported something similar? And if these roots were growing as part of the foundation, what was I supposed to do about them? Leave them there? Fat chance of selling the house! Who the hell wanted a tree molded to the foundation? But maybe it wasn't still growing. Maybe those roots had died after all. Perhaps I'd imagined that one squirming in my hand.

I clung on to the stair rail as I made my way down, sure I heard dragging noises, but rationalizing that had to be impossible.

I looked up. The door was wide open. Terry would be back soon anyway, although I had no idea how long it took to dig a couple of trenches.

At the bottom of the stairs, I inched my way to the corner, where the roots coiled Medusa-like. Thinner, but far more numerous than they'd appeared last time I was down there. If roots were supposed to supply their tree with nutrients, these seemed to have wandered seriously off course. I stared at them, a part of me wanting to touch them again, but scared that if I did, I would experience a similar reaction to the time before. They looked alive. I supposed a dead one would look like kindling, dry to the touch. Easily snapped off. These looked far too supple for that.

The sound of footsteps coming closer hitched my breath in my throat.

Terry, clomping down the stairs. "Oh, sorry, Mrs. Chambers, I didn't mean to startle you."

I backed away from the roots and forced a smile. "Not at all, Terry. I was wondering if these are still alive. If they're still growing."

"Oh, they're alive all right and I've traced their source. At least, I think I have. I dug three or four quick, shallow trenches and they do seem to be related to that tree by the river. I would have to confirm it and none of my colleagues will believe me, but I'm as sure as I can be. *These* roots belong to that tree, and they're still growing."

I stared at him. "But how? And what are they feeding on? There's nothing in here except rubbish, dust and…" I gazed around me at the broken bits of furniture that hadn't made it upstairs. "It's just a cellar."

Terry sighed. "I know. I think you might be wise to call in a building surveyor. They look at things from a different perspective, so with their view as well, you'll be able to start deciding what, if anything, you want to do."

"What if I do nothing?"

Terry shrugged his shoulders. "My guess is that, although the roots are still growing, they're doing so very slowly. As you say, there's nothing for them to feed on. As far as the tree's concerned, there's no obvious benefit to it to have those roots there. The thing that's confusing me is that nature doesn't usually do something without a cause. At least, that's how I understand it anyway. Would you mind if I took some photos? I'd like to send them to the association I belong to. Maybe someone else has seen something like this and can advise what to do."

"Of course. Please. Help yourself."

Terry practically ran up the stairs. Probably wanted to make sure he got his pictures before I changed my mind.

I stared at the roots. "What are you doing here?" I heard myself say. "What do you want?"

Something brushed my leg through my jeans. I looked down—one of the thinner roots had curled around my foot. But surely that hadn't been so close. Had I somehow slid under it? I withdrew my foot and the root hung an inch or two off the ground for a few seconds before settling back on the floor. I stared at it and swallowed hard. I could ask Terry if tree roots moved like that, but I risked looking stupid. Or paranoid. No. I'd already done enough of that with the drama group. I didn't need to become the laughing stock of the Arborists' Association or whatever they called themselves.

Terry reappeared, complete with digital camera. He snapped away for a minute or two, capturing the growth from every angle.

"Would you hold these roots aside for me a second? I want to photograph where they're coming in."

In my present state of mind, that was the last thing I could do. "How about if you hold them back and I take the photo? I said.

"Okay, if you wish. If you could get in really close, that would be great."

He pulled the roots aside and I bent down.

A whooshing noise, like a sigh, filled our corner of the cellar.

Terry jumped. I gasped and nearly dropped the camera. "What was that?"

Terry's face had paled. "Haven't a clue. Wind in the pipes or something?"

I snapped the picture. The flash lit up the wall, illuminating the strange, veined appearance of the bricks.

"*Fuck!*" Terry dropped the cluster of roots he was holding and clasped his wrist, Blood dripped between his fingers.

"Oh my God. What happened?"

"The damn thing scratched me."

The way he described it made it sound like a willful act. His blanched face and open-mouthed expression told me that's exactly how it had felt.

"Let's get you up to the kitchen," I said. "See how bad it is. I have a first-aid kit up there."

It proved to be a superficial wound, deep enough to bleed profusely for a few minutes, but didn't seem to have penetrated anything major. Terry ran it under the cold faucet until the blood stopped. I wrapped his arm in a clean tea towel before dressing it. His hands were shaking.

He glanced up at the clock. "I'll have to go, Mrs. Chambers. I really must get to that other job. See what the surveyor says when you get one. But, as far as I'm concerned, unless I hear anything to the contrary from anyone in the association, my advice would be to leave well alone."

I thanked him, told him to send me the bill, which he said wasn't necessary, and saw him out. I felt sure he never wanted to hear another word about my cellar, or the tree. When Terry Watson left, he was terrified.

Chapter Eight

I can't explain why I went back down to the cellar that day. Part of me wanted only to run away, as fast and as far as my legs would take me. Part of me screamed at my stubborn other self to leave that house. No more shillyshallying. Abandon it and throw away the key. After all, I had no ties anywhere these days. True I'd had some friends from my pre-inheritance days, but it was amazing how many of them had turned out to be less than friends, more like acquaintances. When I told them of my "good fortune", some expressions changed from delight to greed. People I had known for years, and even trusted, were ringing me up, coming to see me, working the conversation around to telling me about some lost cause of theirs, some hardship they had never thought to share with me before. All cost money. I gave willingly at first until I realized that once the money landed in their bank accounts, they drifted off, with barely a "thank you". We no longer had anything in common. So much for friendship.

When my last so-called friend joined their ranks, my disillusion with people hit rock bottom. She already had my change of address, but I didn't inform any of the others. When I left my old life, I left it for good. Only Neil seemed to have followed me and he'd probably asked her for my address. Hopefully that one visit would be his last here, so now I could end my previous life altogether. As I thought about it, I realized I had no regrets about that.

I stood at the top of the cellar steps and stared down. A strange, tugging sensation drew me to place my foot on the first step. My rational side screamed at me to stop. It carried on screaming, louder and louder with each descending step.

The brick walls seemed to close in on me. My sandaled feet echoed on the wooden treads. The hollowness of the sound felt unnatural, as if I had entered some vaulted stone chamber, not this flat-ceilinged cellar.

At the bottom, the earthy, woody smell assaulted me, stronger than before. I had to go there. I had to go up to the tree roots. I didn't know why.

They seemed bunched up even tighter than a few minutes earlier. One or two long, thin tentacles stretched out across the uneven dirt floor. I crept up to the wall at the farthest reach of the root span, where Terry and I had taken the photographs.

My fingers prickled and tingled. I rubbed my hands together, but I had to see the bricks behind the roots; that strange, vein-like construction I had glimpsed when the camera flashed. The warning voice in my head reached fever pitch, but the compulsion to find out what lay there proved far stronger. I stretched out my fingers. They trembled. I stretched them farther. I touched a clump of roots and licked dry lips. The roots rustled in my hand. I swallowed my revulsion as they squirmed like rough maggots, tickling my palm. Gently, I drew them away from the wall, but I couldn't see clearly. Too much shadow. I cursed my stupidity in not bringing the flashlight. I could go back and get it from the stairs where it lay but I knew if I let go now, I probably wouldn't have the courage to try again. I would have to make do.

I moved in closer. There were the bricks—red, rough, and covered in a threadwork pattern of dark brown strands. I touched them, followed their trail up and down the wall. Some seemed to end, achieving no purpose. Others grew broader and thickened out into the roots I held in one hand. Every time I saw them, they had reconfigured themselves.

Something rough and sinewy gripped my hand and I cried out. I shook my fingers and the roots fell away. They settled back against the wall, as they had done before. The warning voice sounded in my head again. It was as if they deliberately arranged themselves. As if some sentient life was choreographing them.

Oh, for pity's sake!

I shivered. It had grown colder, probably because the time was getting late. I moved away and turned my back on the roots. As I reached the stairs, a chill breeze behind me ruffled my hair. I spun around. Out of the corner of my eye, I caught a glimpse. Something tall, dark, arms outstretched at right angles to its body.

A memory stirred.

What had Neil said he'd seen?

A scarecrow.

After Monday, my senses were finely tuned to any sign of pity or ridicule, however well concealed. But the drama group was charming, as before. They greeted me with warm friendliness and behaved as if nothing had happened. Only Shona showed any sign of concern.

"Are you all right?" she asked, as she arrived, alone.

I took her coat. "I'm fine. Really." If I said it enough, maybe I'd convince myself. "I still can't explain the girl Cynthia says she saw, but apart from that, I think I'm getting somewhere." Really? Who was I kidding?

Shona smiled. Did she believe me? She put her hand on my arm and our eyes met. Why had I never noticed before? She had such clear green eyes. Like emeralds. Hypnotizing. "Well that's good news," she said. "Have you moved back in yet?"

"Yes. Today."

Why had I said that? I still had a night's booking at the hotel. Earlier today I had made my mind up to leave this house. The trip to the cellar had changed something. Even with the strange apparition I had thought I'd seen, the rational side of me had been quashed. Inexplicably, I experienced an overwhelming urge to stay. At least for now.

I made tea and added my last packets of chocolate digestives and gypsy creams to a plate. Another rehearsal tomorrow. I'd have to go shopping.

Upstairs, Shona was in full swing as Griselda Clement. I didn't want to disrupt the flow so I hung around outside the rehearsal room, listening for a moment when the director paused the proceedings. I set the tray down on a table. The corridor was quiet, still and dark as the landing light only illuminated the first few feet. Farther along, a bulb was out and I made a mental note to replace it in the morning. Beyond that, the corridor was shrouded and shadowy.

Something dashed across my peripheral vision and a giggle sounded from close by. I peered into the darkness. Nothing. Another giggle. Behind me this time. I turned. Another bulb had burned out and I could see little in the gloom. Down the corridor a door opened, a shaft of light flashed across the floor in front of it. The door closed. The light vanished. And so had she. Veronica. For a split second I had seen her clearly—blonde plaits, yellow dress, happy smile.

And she had seen me.

My heart thumped. My mouth dried. I heard chatter from the other side of the door. The cast had taken their break. Without a word, I opened the door, picked up the tray, and took it inside.

"Oh, lovely," said Shona, handing out the biscuits. "Gypsy creams. My favorites."

The plate emptied in seconds. My hand shook a little as I poured the tea.

Shona whispered to me. "Are you all right, Maddie? You look a little pale."

"I'm fine. Thank you for asking though."

She didn't look convinced. And another look passed over her face. A strange look I couldn't fathom. As if somehow I couldn't be "fine". Another symptom of my paranoia no doubt. Actually I amazed myself at how calm I felt. And at how I closed the door and left the drama group happily munching and sipping, while I walked steadily down the corridor to the door that had opened a few minutes earlier. I touched the handle and nearly lost my nerve.

I leaned against it, my ear pressed close, straining to pick up any sound, however slight. Nothing. I stepped back and turned the handle, meeting a little resistance at first. Had it been stiff like this before? I pushed harder and it opened, with a creak. Inky darkness met me. I reached for the light switch and pressed it. One dim bulb in the center of the large room did little to illuminate it, but I recognized it instantly. The white sheets, shrouding old, discarded furniture, boxes, pictures.

My nerve deserted me and I backed out of the room, switching the light off and closing the door. A second after I turned away, I heard that giggle again. Veronica's giggle. I looked down at the floor. Light from a much brighter source than the dim bulb was seeping out from the room into the corridor. I struggled to keep calm as I stared at it. The light went off.

I half ran to the stairs. My resolve to stay in the house had evaporated in an instant. I couldn't stay here tonight. I wouldn't get a minute's sleep, and I needed my wits about me. I would stay at the hotel and regain my sanity. Everything would look far clearer in the morning. For one thing, I could get Charlie to come over and fix more lighting in that room, and I'd get some local man-with-a-van to come and clear it out.

As for the cellar. I'd leave that alone. After all, it wasn't doing anyone any harm. If anything, those roots were strengthening the foundation. Somehow.

I lay back against the plump, pristine pillows in my hotel room and poured a miniature of scotch I'd found in the mini-bar into a glass I retrieved from the bathroom. I sipped it while, on TV, an old film played. *The Haunting*.

I usually loved horror films, especially the old ones. I'd lost count of how many times I'd seen this one, but always enjoyed its scary twists and turns, the sudden shocks and hidden demons. But somehow it scared me more that night. And not in that delicious, hide behind the pillow kind of way.

I flicked the remote and found an old romantic musical. Ginger Rogers proving that she really did do everything Fred Astaire did—backward.

My mind wandered back to Hargest House. So much was wrong there. And what bothered me most was my reaction this evening. I'd been compelled to go down to that cellar, when any sane person would have kept the door locked, at least until the surveyor had added his—or her—opinion to Terry's. But even more inexplicable was my decision to investigate *that* room. In the dark. After I'd seen…well, whatever it was I'd seen. Maybe, being on my own too much, my imagination had started to play tricks on me. That was pretty much the only explanation I currently had for the apparent manifestation of my childhood imaginary family. It almost worked too, except I hadn't been the only one to see one of them.

Then there were all the stories about Aunt Charlotte. I racked my brain for memories of her. Most seemed to come from my pre-teen days, with flashes from later years and still nothing from the last year. Aunt Charlotte laughing. Singing with her around that piano. Picnics in the grounds; a red and white checked tablecloth spread out under the tree. The tentacle tree. When I was small enough, I used to climb into its semi-circular hollow. Flashes of conversation came back to me. My eight-year-old self asking question after question.

"When did the lightning strike, Aunt Charlotte?"

"Many years ago, dear. Before Mr. Hargest built this house. Before anyone who is alive today was born."

"Is it as old as Priory St. Michael?"

"Well now, Priory St. Michael is at least a thousand years old. But I think it may be. Or even older."

"Will it be here all my life? 'Til I'm your age?"

Her rich laughter rang out. "I expect so, Maddie. Even when you reach my great age, this tree will still be standing. It's a very special tree."

"It's the tentacle tree. Does it mind me calling it that?"

More laughter. Indulgent this time. "I'm sure it doesn't mind at all."

"Why do you talk to it?"

My eyes shot open. I'd forgotten that. Aunt Charlotte used to talk to the tree. I had seen her—head pressed close up to it, hands outstretched along the branches. I'd never heard what she'd said; her words were whispered, hurried, indecipherable; maybe not even in English. I closed my eyes again and tried to recapture that sunny day, the picnic, her response. But the moment had passed. The memory faded. Somehow I knew I had to remember. The Aunt Charlotte I knew at that time had been different, eccentric even, but she never went in for general tree hugging, or talking to any of the plants in her garden. Not in my hearing anyway. Unless I had forgotten. No. It was *that* tree. I had seen her *Book of Shadows*. Willows were important to her and there was something about *that* willow in particular. It was as entwined into Aunt Charlotte's life as its roots were to the house.

Now her house belonged to me. After so many years' estrangement, she could have left it to anyone and no one would have blamed her. Her will had been dated only last year. A simple single sheet of paper the solicitor had read out to me while I sat, unable to believe what I heard.

To my niece, Madeleine Chambers (née Johnson), I leave my entire estate, including the house and grounds known as Hargest House. She will remember.

Remember what, Aunt Charlotte? And why is it so important that I do?

Chapter Nine

The chill in the rehearsal room hit me at the door. The cast would certainly need those heaters tonight. I rubbed my hands together, pulled my cardigan tighter around my body and flicked the switches on, turning the dials up to maximum.

I hurried out of the freezing room and shut the door behind me. In the distance, the doorbell rang. It should have been the house clearance man with a van. It wasn't.

"Hello, Maddie."

"Charlie. I wasn't expecting you 'til tomorrow."

He grinned and came into the hall. "I finished my last job early, so I thought I'd see if I could make a start now."

"That would be great. I have a man coming to clear all the rubbish out of there, but I'm sure you'll manage to keep out of each other's way."

The smile faded for a second. "You're throwing all your aunt's stuff out?"

"It's only old junk. Broken furniture, that sort of thing. I haven't a clue why it's in there, to be honest. All the other rooms on that floor and the one above are pretty much empty, but that one's a general dumping ground."

The smile returned. "Well, we all need one of those, don't we? Mine's my cellar, but yours is already occupied, isn't it? Thought any more about that tree?"

I followed him up the stairs. "I'll get a surveyor in at some stage. But the arborist seems to think the roots aren't a threat to the foundation."

"Think you'll keep the old place after all?"

We had arrived on the second floor. I hesitated. Had I mentioned my thoughts on selling the house to Charlie? I didn't think so. Maybe he'd read something into my attitude at some stage. Perhaps Shona had told him. Every day found me more confused about what I did want to do. I was frustrated with myself. From being a decisive person, I had turned into a woman who changed her mind every day, and I had no idea why. It felt almost as if my mind wasn't entirely my own anymore. For now, it seemed, I was staying here—but tomorrow could paint a whole different picture.

"I don't know, Charlie. Some days I think I will, and some days I want to sell."

"You should stay here. This house suits you."

"What? You mean old and decrepit?" I laughed.

"No. More dark and mysterious." He laughed too.

I had a question that had been bugging me. One of many in my current confused state of mind. "There's something I've been meaning to ask you, Charlie. Why is your brother Pete so afraid of this floor? He refused to even come up here when I asked him to quote for decorating."

Charlie looked down at his boots. "Pete can be a complete prat at times. I mean, he's my brother and all, but when he gets superstitious, I lose patience with him."

"I've heard the rumors about satanic rituals in this house. I can't believe my aunt would have anything to do with such nonsense."

He met my gaze. "I would never go so far as to say it was nonsense. Too many bizarre things have happened in this town. But Pete is an idiot for turning work down. The old man's long gone and buried and Miss Grant isn't... Oh, I'm sorry, Maddie. I shouldn't pass comment on your aunt."

"By 'the old man', I assume you mean Nathaniel Hargest? Nasty piece of work by all accounts."

"Did your aunt ever mention him to you?"

I shook my head. "Only a little, in passing. He died before I started coming here anyway."

"Memories are long in a small town where people have lived for generations. Stories get passed down, and embellished along the way."

"That's what Shona said. What is it you were going to say about my aunt?" I hoped my smile would encourage him to be candid. It didn't.

"Oh nothing. Just that she isn't with us anymore either."

I stared at him, but nothing else was forthcoming. He'd broken eye contact and the silence was becoming awkward.

We moved on and passed the open door of the rehearsal room. I pulled it shut and remembered. I had closed it earlier, but I couldn't have latched it properly. I gave the handle an extra tug and pushed back on it. It held firm.

"I'm trying to warm that room up. The drama group is here tonight."

"Do you want me to install a couple of radiators in there? If you carry on using those convectors your electricity bills are going to soar."

I thought for a moment. "Yes, please. I think that would be a good idea after all. It'll save a lot of messing about too."

"I'll get onto it tomorrow." He opened the door of the junk room. Oddly this one wasn't as cold as the previous room. It smelled fusty. Damp. I hadn't noticed that before. And there was another smell I couldn't put my finger on.

We agreed where the new light fixtures should go. "I'll leave you to it," I said to Charlie. "Give me a shout when you want a coffee or tea."

The doorbell rang again and a couple of minutes later, the house clearance man followed me up the stairs. I introduced him to Charlie, who was clearing a space for himself at the far end of the room. The sheets he had removed revealed antique chests of drawers, wardrobes and chairs, even an old rocking horse.

"This is Harry, Charlie. He's come to clear all this mess out of your way."

I went back down the stairs, with housework on my mind. The living room needed a really good dusting. Fifteen minutes later, I was polishing Aunt Charlotte's fine, old mahogany table.

Rapid footsteps thudded down the stairs, into the hall. I dashed out, to see Harry looking as if the devil himself was chasing him. He glanced at me and made for the front door, with nothing in his hands.

"I'm sorry, Mrs. Chambers."

I followed him out to his van. "Whatever's the matter?"

He was already climbing into the driver's seat. "That room." He shook his head as if he was trying to rid himself of the memory. "There's something in there. Haven't you seen it? Them?"

Panic reared up inside me. "What are you talking about? Charlie's up there. Just Charlie." Who was I trying to convince? Harry or me?

Harry stared at me, slammed his door shut and started up his engine, crunching the gears. His window was open and I grabbed it. "Please, tell me. What did you see up there that scared you so much?"

He hesitated, stared at me for a second as if about to say something. But nothing came. He shook his head and looked away. The van began to move and I dropped my hands. He gave me one last look. Surprisingly, I read pity in his eyes. His tires squealed. He couldn't wait to get out of there. First Terry, now Harry. Both had been scared witless by something in my house. Charlie was still up there. Maybe he could tell me what had scared the poor man.

He climbed down off his ladder. "I'm as baffled as you are," he said, as he selected a smaller screwdriver. "Pleasant enough chap. Don't think he's local, is he?"

"He's from Rokesby Green. I found him online."

Charlie nodded. "He'd made a start, as you can see." He pointed to a tidy pile of old and threadbare curtains, next to some furniture which had been reduced to firewood, ready for transportation downstairs.

"He was smashing away there with his hammer and then he suddenly stopped and backed away. I asked him what was wrong and he didn't say a word. He just pointed at the cupboard over there."

I glanced over at the recently unveiled tall wardrobe. Maybe Charlie's presence gave me courage but, without thinking, I marched over to it and flung the doors open.

Empty. Nothing but a bad smell. Like rotten eggs. Sulfur. I covered my nose and slammed the doors shut, "Oh God, that's awful. That's what I could smell in here earlier. What's caused that?"

Charlie shrugged. "It *is* nasty, isn't it? I'm afraid I haven't a clue."

"Well I'm going to have to find out and get rid of it." I examined the outside of the wardrobe. Still the foul stench polluted the air, though not as strong now the doors were shut again. It was like any other, ugly, freestanding piece of early twentieth century bedroom furniture. Dark wood of indeterminate origin, standing a few inches off the floor on four, solid rectangular feet. It towered a good couple of feet above me.

"I can't understand how that smell could have got in there," I said, as I peered at one side of the wardrobe. It stood a good six inches from the wall. "Maybe Aunt Charlotte kept something in there that went bad and the smell lingered. I suppose if no one's opened it in a long time, it's possible."

"That's probably it," Charlie said, climbing his ladder again. "Anyway, the smell's almost gone now."

"Or maybe we've grown used to it."

He gave a quick smile. Gone almost before it had begun.

"*You* haven't seen anything…odd, have you?"

"Not a thing. Apart from that chap's behavior. That was definitely strange."

"Thanks, Charlie. I'll let you get on."

As I passed the rehearsal room door I closed it and went back to my dusting. A wafting aroma of cigarette smoke drifted past my nose. I stopped polishing, heard a masculine cough behind me and turned. On the edge of my vision, something moved so fast I couldn't be sure I'd seen it. But somehow I knew I had. And something told me I recognized it—however impossible it might seem. Tom.

My hands trembled so much I dropped the duster. My mouth dried up so I could barely swallow.

Charlie was in the house. I wasn't alone. I must remember that. And later, the drama group would be coming. The house would be filled with noise. Laughter. Chatter. Normality.

In the kitchen, I poured a glass of water and stared out of the window. The willow tree had shed almost all its leaves, and it was naked. Vulnerable.

A sudden whining of rusty hinges made me jump and I turned to see the cellar door swinging open.

Whispers. Coming from down below. I had nowhere to run, except outside. And then where? I must get past the door. Back into the hall.

I set the glass down on the draining board and forced one reluctant foot in front of the other, moving silently. The door was a few feet away to my left, half open. The whispering grew louder, the closer I came. Childish whispers, and a couple of older ones, their words indistinct. In a few seconds, I would pass them. I readied myself. I put my hand to the door and flung it with all my strength. It slammed shut, the noise echoing through the hall. I ran to the stairs and sat down on them, hugging myself and rocking back and forth, trembling.

I'd heard one clear word. A name. The name they would use for me if they were real.

Kelly.

Shona followed me out of the rehearsal room as the cast enjoyed their break. I was halfway down the stairs when she spoke. "Let's go and have a little chat in the living room. They don't need me for the rest of the rehearsal. I can see something's wrong and I want to help. Will you let me?"

I looked into her clear green eyes. Here, surely, was a woman I could trust.

"Yes, please. I need to tell someone. You see, I think, somehow, they've come alive."

She recoiled as if I'd slapped her, but recovered herself. There was no going back. I told her everything, ending with, "I'm certifiably crazy, aren't I?"

Shona had listened patiently throughout. Now she sat back and raised her eyes. "What's that famous expression of Sherlock Holmes? 'When you have eliminated the impossible, whatever remains, *however improbable*, must be the truth'? Perhaps that applies here. We know there was no one but you and us cast members that night, so no one could have directed Cynthia to the bathroom, but she is adamant that someone did. More than that, she is positive that the description she gave was an accurate one. She's mentioned it more than once since. You say it fits this imaginary sister of yours and that you have seen the younger one—Veronica—more than once?"

I nodded. "And then there's the cigarette smoke."

"But you've not actually seen the boy—Tom?"

"I'm not sure. I thought I saw something earlier tonight. In here."

"Maddie, in my life I've seen and heard all sorts of things. Believe me, your story isn't half as strange as some. A few of the people who've left those flats in the High Street told me the most extraordinary tales."

"The black dog? I think I may have seen it a few days ago when I went up the High Street, shopping."

"And did it have blazing red eyes?"

"No, but it looked like no breed of dog I've ever seen. And it was big. I mean, we're talking St. Bernard proportions here but with some features I've never seen before. The eyes were piercing, not doleful as so many dogs' are. And its haunches…the muscles were bulging." I shuddered at the memory. "I was on the other side of the street to it. It stared at me. Even when I'd passed it, I knew it was watching me."

She smiled and gazed into the distance. "I must be the only one in Priory St. Michael not to have seen it. Now why would that be, do you think? Who's to say? Only the dog, presumably and he's not talking." She laughed, in a vain attempt to lift my mood I was sure.

"I think what I'm saying, Maddie, is that I have learned enough in my time to keep an open mind about anything that cannot be readily explained. You've had some scares, but has anything actually threatened you?"

I didn't answer straightaway. I thought over all the strange events, half-sightings, the whispering from the cellar, the doors that seemed to open by themselves, those damn roots. Shona was right. Despite everything, nothing had threatened me.

"No. Frightened me half to death though. And scared the life out of my ex-husband, a tree surgeon and a house clearance man." I managed a light laugh.

"Your ex-husband?"

Of course, I hadn't told Shona about Neil's uninvited, nocturnal visit. I didn't want to get into a long conversation about it now either.

"Oh, he turned up, wanting to get back with me—or my money, more like. I sent him away, but not before he'd allegedly had a close encounter with something he couldn't explain. The trouble with Neil is I never know when to believe him or not. Mostly I've learned to treat everything he says as suspect. Honesty was never one of his strengths." I managed a light laugh. "But I have to confess, this time he did seem genuinely upset."

"I think we have to be open to the possibility that you and he really did see and hear those things. The question remains why?"

"Have you any ideas?"

Shona shook her head. "Not one, I'm afraid." She paused. "Charlie's lived here all his life and he's a sensible sort of chap. Maybe have a word with him about anything he knows about this house. His reaction when you asked him about Pete shows he's not one to give way to superstition and hearsay."

The sound of chatter came from the hall. The rehearsal was breaking up for the night.

Shona looked at her watch. "Good gracious, is that the time?" She stood. "Try not to worry, Maddie. I'm sure we'll get to the bottom of it. But I won't promise a logical explanation this time. I know better than that."

I followed her out into the hall. Most of the cast had already left. A chilly blast of air blew through the open door. "October's with us all right," Shona said as I helped her on with her coat. "It'll be Christmas before we know where we are. I see the shops have got their Halloween paraphernalia out already."

Halloween. The thought of it set my heart pounding.

I settled in bed for my first night's sleep at Hargest House since Sunday. I reached to switch off the lamp but stopped. Somehow I couldn't bring myself to plunge into total blackness. Tiredness overwhelmed me and my eyes closed. I pulled the duvet close around my shoulders to keep out the chill in the room. Apart from the cheerful, warming fires here in my childhood, I'd always been brought up to sleep in a cool, if not cold, bedroom. Overheated rooms kept me awake.

A sudden noise jolted me from my near-sleep state. It came from overhead. Something had fallen down upstairs. I should go and investigate. I sat up. No, whatever it was would surely keep 'til morning. I lay back down again. Closed my eyes.

The crash was louder this time. I shot up in bed.

My mind raced with possible explanations. An intruder. In which case, investigating could be dangerous. I should call the police. I scanned the room, flinching at the shadows in dark corners, not illuminated by my bedside lamp. Silvery fingers of moonlight pierced the gaps between the curtains. I realized I was holding my breath and exhaled, wishing my breathing didn't make so much noise.

I cursed silently. My phone was in my purse, downstairs in the living room. In future I must remember to bring it up with me when I went to bed. Fat lot of good that would do me now though.

I listened. Minutes ticked by. I got out of bed, went to the closed door and put my ear against it. Nothing. Above me was the junk room. Maybe Harry hadn't stacked the stuff too well and it had worked loose and toppled over. Yes, that was it. Surely after all this time, any intruder would have realized there was nothing worth stealing on the upper floors and have made his way down. The key was in the lock and I turned it. He would have to break the door down to get to me. I lost track of time as my feet and legs grew colder by the second.

Not a sound.

Nothing was going to make me turn that key until daylight. Tomorrow I would also arm myself with something I could defend myself with. A baseball bat. Or a cricket bat maybe. Those umbrellas of Aunt Charlotte's had vicious spikes, but they were so old, they were falling apart.

I was shivering. As certain as I could be that I wasn't about to be killed in my own home, I climbed back into bed and pulled the covers tightly around me. Eventually, sheer exhaustion overcame me and I slept for a couple of hours.

I awoke at eight thirty. A gray, rain-soaked morning greeted me as I pulled back the drapes. I was hit by the feeling of profound sadness I always felt when autumn began taking its inevitable toll of the weather, leaving dankness and death in its wake. With a sigh, I moved away from the window.

By the time Charlie arrived, I was showered, dressed and drinking coffee, but still hadn't plucked up courage to go and find out what had caused the crashes the night before. I'd almost managed to convince myself I'd dreamed it. Almost.

Charlie went upstairs and I followed. At least with him in the house, I felt less vulnerable to whatever I would find when I opened that door. Charlie disappeared into the rehearsal room, while I summoned up every ounce of courage I could muster and turned the door handle of the junk room.

I scoured the room for any sign of disturbance but, with everything in such a mess anyway, how would I know? Harry's cleared area looked the same as before. For the first time, I paid close attention to the individual items that were stacked and strewn around the untidy room. The old, broken rocking horse leaned drunkenly up against one wall, the paint cracked and peeling. Try as I might, I couldn't remember ever playing with it. It was probably broken even when I was a child. That appeared to be the only child's toy and I wondered fleetingly who had owned it. Surely there had been no other children in this house but me? As I approached it, I saw the rockers were broken, hence the odd angle. No one had played with this in a very long time. Maybe it had been a favorite toy of Aunt

Charlotte's and she had brought it with her. Maybe it had belonged to Nathaniel Hargest himself when he was a boy.

Then I saw it—the wardrobe that had given off the sulfurous stench. It lay, face down. That's what I must have heard crashing to the floor. I picked my way around it. There was no smell now and I could see the back, sides and feet. Solid, heavy wood. How could something so big and heavy have toppled over? Unless someone strong had pushed it.

Something glinted and distracted my attention. A tall, cheval mirror, partially covered by a sheet which I pulled across. Like others in this room, the glass was crazed and mottled, but otherwise it looked in good condition. My reflection stared back at me. I looked tired, and in need of a good night's sleep. My eyes appeared dull and lusterless, my lips dry and pale. I pushed my untidy hair behind my ears and blinked.

My vision blurred. I blinked again. The image in the mirror swam before my eyes. I stared at the impossible. Looking back at me wasn't my adult face. It was me as a child. But not the shy child I had been. This child stared out at the world with confidence and assuredness. Her blue eyes blinked steadily, shining and clear. Her long chestnut hair lay thick and straight, like a shawl around her shoulders, gleaming as mine never did. Her perfect button nose and sculpted lips with their natural rose tint. All were familiar. All my imperfections perfected. My antithesis and my ideal. I knew her. I had created her from my own imagination. She was everything I had aspired to be. Kelly.

Behind her, shadows swirled.

Over to my right, the gramophone crackled and hissed as the scratchy first chords of "Serenade in Blue" started to play. I saw the record spinning on the turntable, even though I knew it couldn't. The machine hadn't been wound up in years. Even if it had, that record was in no fit condition to play.

A young woman's voice whispered in my ear. "The devil's serenade…"

The music stopped. The turntable was still. The door slammed, but I ignored it. My attention was all on the vision in the mirror. The child's lips twitched, then broke into a smile. She put her right forefinger to her lips. I couldn't have spoken anyway. At that moment, I doubted my voice would have made a sound if my life depended on it.

I wanted to run. God knows, I wanted to get out of there as fast as I could, but my feet wouldn't work. I willed my hands to flex, but they stayed, rigid, at my sides. Something held me there, fast. I couldn't even move my head. Beads of sweat formed on my forehead and coursed down my cheeks. I was straining as hard as I could to get some muscles working. None obeyed.

A scream formed in my mind, but my mouth stayed stubbornly shut and the scream only echoed through the chambers of my brain.

Out of the shadows behind the girl, a face took shape. A young woman. Shoulder length red-brown hair, dark eye shadow, shell-pink lips, and a serious expression. Thelma. So they were all here, in one way or another. Even my own alter ego.

The unmistakable scent of Opium wafted into my nostrils.

Kelly had gone, and I stared back at myself. Thelma moved off to one side. I staggered.

At last, my muscles obeyed me and I could move.

A creaking sounded behind me. The rocking horse no longer leaned against the wall. It moved steadily back and forth, as if someone was riding it. I looked down; the rockers were still broken. Part of one was missing, yet the thing still rocked. I heard a giggle—the same one I had heard before. The giggle that couldn't belong to Veronica but somehow did.

I raced out of the room and slammed the door. Charlie emerged from the rehearsal room. He frowned. "Is everything all right, Maddie?"

I was panting. I nodded. I couldn't tell him what had happened.

"You look really pale. Shall I get you a cup of tea?"

"No, honestly. I'm fine. Really. I've been sorting some stuff out, a bit too energetically I think. I'll be okay in a minute. I need to catch my breath."

Charlie continued to stare at me, with concern in his eyes. "I need to pop down to the cellar and check the fuse box."

"Fine," I said and forced a smile, hoping it didn't look as false as I feared. I followed him downstairs. My heart only stopped thumping painfully when we arrived in the kitchen.

The doorbell rang. Shona stood on the doorstep, dripping wet. Her breath made clouds.

I opened the door wide to let her in and a chill breeze followed her. At least I could explain that. I forced myself to make polite conversation. "The weather's turned really cold today, hasn't it?" I said, taking her wet parka. I hung it over the banister and she followed me into the kitchen.

"At least you're nice and cozy here."

"Thanks to Charlie Evans. He's in the cellar at the moment, but he's fixing a couple of new radiators in the rehearsal room. Should be much warmer than with the convectors."

"Oh, lovely." She frowned. "You don't look very well. Did you get any sleep last night?"

"Not much." I shook my head and tears pricked my eyes.

Shona put her hand on my arm. "Let's have a cup of tea and you can tell me about it."

My hands shook as I filled the kettle. She took it off me and did the job herself. I called down to Charlie in the cellar to ask if he wanted some tea but he declined. His voice sounded far away. Once again, the dank smell penetrated the atmosphere, and I shivered.

I closed the cellar door.

Shona had made her way to the living room with our tea. I followed her, casting a quick glance up the stairs as I passed.

"It's happened again," I said. "Only this time I saw myself as a child—I mean as the child I wanted to be all those years ago. The one I called Kelly. And I saw my imaginary eldest sister, Thelma. An old gramophone started to play a record all by itself. Not only that, last night, a heavy wardrobe crashed to the floor."

Shona took a sip of tea and looked thoughtful. Did she believe me? In her position, I'm not sure I would have.

"I can see you're really stressed right now," she said.

I put my head in my hands. "I just wish it would stop."

Shona set her mug down on a small table by her side. "It wouldn't be unheard of for the stress itself to be causing hallucinations. You were happy with your imaginary family when you were a child, weren't you?"

I looked up. "Yes, but it's the strange things I keep seeing and hearing that are causing the stress."

But Shona had latched on to something and she wasn't about to let go. "Moving house—especially the way you did, leaving pretty much everything and everyone behind—is one of the most stressful experiences anyone can have. Your whole life changed with your aunt's inheritance. You've had to deal with your ex-husband turning up and clearly wanting to get his hands on your money. It's bound to drag things up from the past. I'm no psychologist, but I'm sure it wouldn't be unheard of for your brain to search for a happier time and set of circumstances and console you with them."

"So you're saying I'm making all this up?" I couldn't remove the indignant edge to my voice.

"No, no, not in the way you mean. To you it's all too real."

"But if it's my mind that's creating the images for me, how did Cynthia see Sonia that time? And how did that wardrobe fall over?"

Shona sighed. "That's where my argument breaks down." She held her hands up.

"I haven't a clue. It's the one thing I can't explain. I do know Cynthia had treatment for schizophrenia some time ago and is probably still on medication for it. Maybe she imagined it."

"Maybe," I said. "I know nothing about schizophrenia." I tapped my forehead. "I still can't remember anything from that last summer when I was sixteen."

The door opened. I jumped. Charlie stood there. "You're nervy," he said, smiling. "I came to tell you I'm all done for today. I'll be back tomorrow first thing. There's something a bit strange though."

My heart sank. I could do without any more shocks. "What is it, Charlie?"

"In the cellar. I think you'd better come and see."

I cast a pleading look at Shona. "I'll come too," she said, to my relief. "My curiosity would never forgive me if I didn't."

Down in the cellar, Charlie turned at the bottom of the stairs. I gasped at the sight in front of me. The tree roots had grown from their original position, extending a few feet from the wall. They practically filled one corner of the cellar and had bushed out. Long, woody tentacles reached out along the floor.

"They must have sprouted a good three or four feet since I was last down here," Charlie said.

I looked at Shona. She stared at the roots. "I've never seen anything like that in my life," she said. "Aren't they affecting the foundation at all?"

I grasped the nearest clump of root material and pulled it away from the wall, forcing myself to ignore the unpleasant sensation of maggots writhing in my hands.

"Can you shine the flashlight over here, Charlie?"

He picked it up off the stairs and returned within seconds. A bright beam of light lit up the bricks, revealing the veins of tentacles permeating them.

Shona gasped. "How on earth is that possible?"

I dropped the roots, glad to be rid of them. They settled back, as they had before.

"I have no idea," I said. "Charlie?"

"Not a clue," he said, after a moment's hesitation when I thought he hadn't heard me.

That hesitation bothered me. I could have sworn something had triggered in Charlie's mind. Something he wasn't prepared to share with us.

"Well I'd better get going," he said, and I knew I wasn't imagining the speed with which he packed away his tools and left. I wasn't the only one who noticed it either.

"He was in a hurry all of a sudden, wasn't he?" Shona said.

"Did you see his reaction when I asked him if he knew anything that could cause the roots to behave and grow like that?"

Shona shook her head.

"I think Charlie knows something he's not telling me. Maybe to do with this house. I mean, he was in the junk room when Harry, the house clearance man, was spooked. Yet he said nothing happened.

But something must have happened, Shona. The man tore out of here like the devil himself was on his tail."

Shona shivered. Or was it a shudder?

After she left, I made my way back into the kitchen. I looked at the cellar door and imagined the roots down there, silently creeping farther along the floor. What would happen when they reached the stairs? It was my turn to shudder.

Chapter Ten

Charlie returned the next morning but seemed perplexed when I questioned him about the previous day. In the end, I dropped the subject. He finished the job, promising to return the following week to fit some much-needed sockets in the living room.

Meanwhile, I slept each night with my door locked and a newly acquired cricket bat in easy reach. It gave me comfort having something to defend myself with, although it would provide scant defense against anything of a supernatural origin. A new determination had taken hold of me. This was *my* house. Why should I allow something that seemed to have sprung from my imagination push me out of it? The more I thought about it, the more I was convinced my problems with Hargest House could be laid firmly at the door of whatever happened to me that summer I turned sixteen. If I needed to remember and finally deal with whatever that was, I was only going to be able to do it here. So, here I must stay.

Three days went by. Quiet, peaceful, uneventful. I went shopping in the town. I even managed to talk to people and strike up conversations with strangers without having to imagine myself as confident Kelly. In fact, since I'd seen her reflection in the mirror, I preferred not to think about her.

I avoided the frosty woman in the convenience store and discovered a small supermarket around the corner. I didn't say who I was. If they knew, they didn't say. The cashiers and I passed the time of day and exchanged pleasantries about the state of the weather. Not much more, but it was a start. Walking back down the street, I looked over at the newly erected scaffolding along the front of the condemned apartment block on the High Street.

An elderly woman caught me staring at it. "The sooner that's down the better. Nothing good will ever come of building there. They might as well level it off and leave it for nature to take over. That's if anything would grow in that accursed soil."

"Do you live here?"

"All my life." Her pale blue eyes searched mine. "And while they're at it, they should take down that evil man's house." To my dismay, she pointed down the hill.

"You mean Hargest House?"

She nodded. "Evil. He built evil into that house. My grandmother remembered the first time he came here. Nathaniel Hargest. As wicked a man as ever walked the earth. He took lives, and worse than that."

"What could be worse than that?"

She leaned closer to me. "He took their souls."

I stared at her. She nodded. "And he had an accomplice. That Charlotte Grant."

I could feel the color draining from my face. The woman seemed about to say more, but her expression changed. She backed away from me. "Who are you?"

"Maddie Chambers. I live in Hargest House."

She gave a little cry and set off down the hill, moving much more quickly than I would have thought her capable of. Anything to get away from me as fast as her eighty-something-year-old legs would carry her.

I stared after her. If only I'd learned more. I didn't even know her name.

Shona did though. "I think you may mean Mrs. Lloyd. Kathleen Lloyd. She lives in the sheltered housing complex. She must be eighty-eight if she's a day. Nice lady most of the time. Bit fierce sometimes."

"She frightened the life out of me."

Shona smiled. "She's quite a local character. Famous for saying what she thinks, without necessarily considering the impact of her words beforehand. She had a best friend for years, a Mrs. Webster. They used to go to bingo together, whist drives, all that sort of stuff. Fell out over something neither of them could remember and never spoke again. Mrs. Webster died last year and I heard Kathleen refused point blank to go to the funeral."

"Maybe she thought it would be hypocritical."

"Possibly."

"Shona, do you know her to speak to? Judging by the way she raced off when she found out who I was, I won't be able to get anything out of her, but you'd be doing me a massive favor if you could. Would you ask her what she remembers about this house? Why she told me Nathaniel Hargest took souls as well as lives? And why she referred to my aunt as his accomplice? I mean that would make her as evil as he was, and I'm having a hard time believing that."

Shona looked stunned for a moment, then quickly recovered herself. "I'll certainly do my best, although we're not exactly friends. I know where she lives. How are you managing here?"

I crossed my fingers. "It seems to have gone quiet at the moment, so I'm hanging on. I feel I've got to deal with whatever's locked away in my head and not let it beat me." I sounded a lot more confident than I felt.

"Well, *we* really appreciate your help. Goodness knows where we'd be without that room, especially now it's gone so cold and you've got that heating in. It's made all the difference."

When Shona left, I fancied a walk. The weather was crisp, cold, but sunny and I decided to go down by the river. My coat kept out the drafts and my boots and gloves made sure my feet and hands were warm. Outside, a few remaining dry, brown leaves fluttered down from the trees, adding to the mulch I now squelched through.

I was deep in thought when I reached the tentacle tree. I stopped and peered up through its denuded branches as I removed my glove and ran my hand along the gnarled and scarred bark. At ground level, the roots disappeared beneath the pile of dead leaves. I scraped at them with my foot, clearing a small patch of bare earth. The roots looked like those of any other tree.

"Only yours aren't, are they?" I suddenly realized I had spoken my thoughts. Good job no one was around.

A faint breeze caressed my cheek like a cool hand. My fingers tingled. Faint at first, quickly gaining strength. The branch I was stroking suddenly bent and I jumped back. The breeze stroked my face again and brought with it a whisper.

"Kelly…"

I cried out. My whole body shook as if a bolt of lightning had struck me. A few yards away, closer to the house, stood the tall figure of a man, dressed in a long black coat, and wearing a top hat which he raised to me. The faintest of smiles curled his lips. As I stayed there, unable to move, he turned and walked steadily toward the house. Then, as if he had stepped through some invisible door, he disappeared.

The tree rustled; withered leaves around me swirled. Still I stood, rigid, and they settled. There was no wind. No breeze. But the branches bent, until the tree was leaning over even farther than usual. A sudden gust blew me back. I tripped, fell, struggled to my feet. The gale blasted the tree. Its gnarled branches creaked and bent. But all around me remained still. Only around the tree did the wind howl.

It stopped as suddenly as it had begun. Birds sang and I realized that this too had ceased all the time the bizarre tempest had raged.

I backed away. Where could I go? The man seemed so familiar. Too familiar. If I went back to the house, would I see him there? The very thought of him terrified me.

Somewhere deep in my brain a memory stirred. As if one of those infernal shutters had begun to lift and, as it did so, a cloud of darkness and dread filled my body and soul.

I staggered back to the house without seeing the strange man. My fingers trembled so much I dropped the house keys twice. Finally I opened the door. The hall seemed warm and inviting—a whole world away from what I had experienced. I listened, hardly daring to breathe, terrified the man had invaded my house. But he'd disappeared before he reached the front door.

I set the keys down on the hall table and took off my coat, draping it over the banister.

I might need that again at short notice.

In the kitchen, the clock ticked. A tap dripped—I turned it slightly and it stopped. I tried the cellar door. Locked. The man couldn't have got into the house. Not if he was *human* anyway. He was so familiar. I was sure I'd seen him somewhere before. In this house. I crossed over the hall into the living room. I had seen an old photograph album in Aunt Charlotte's bureau, under the bay window. I opened the top drawer. There it lay, right on top.

I set the album on the table and opened it. Shots of me as a child, playing in the garden here. The memories flooded back. A young Aunt Charlotte. Younger than I remembered her, in black and white, impossible to tell the color of her hair, but probably that familiar ash blonde, or light brown like mine used to be before I discovered gray hairs and started giving nature a helping hand.

Aunt Charlotte's clear eyes stared out at me. Her ring-less hands were clasped lightly in her lap. Next to her stood an occasional table with a bowl of roses on it. But there was something else. I peered closer. There was a photograph in a frame that could have been silver. An older man. My heart beat quicker.

I turned the pages of the photo album, past color pictures of my parents, smiling and happy. They gazed at each other, oblivious to their small child, playing with her doll on the carpet in front of them. That must have been a day when they were either dropping me off or picking me back up. My mother was dressed in a sleeveless, white summer dress that showed off her tan. My father wore a T-shirt and jeans. I lingered over that photograph for a long time. I could almost remember that time, but I could have been no more than nine or ten, if that.

I turned another page and froze. These pictures were in no kind of order. The 1970s gave way to the 1950s, or maybe earlier. The photograph was black and white. The man who stared out at me wore a long black coat and a top hat. One hand clasped a silver handled walking stick. My eyes fixed on that face. I had only seen it a few minutes earlier. Yet the owner had been dead for forty-five years. Aunt Charlotte had written beneath it in her neat hand: *The devil, Nathaniel Hargest*.

The chill breeze I had felt before in this room, brushed my face. A small child's voice rang out.

"Kelly."

I ran. Out of the room. Up to my bedroom. This time I grabbed the largest suitcase and threw open the wardrobe and drawers. I piled everything in. I grabbed toiletries from the bathroom and threw them in too. I could barely shut the case, but I didn't care. To hell with facing my demons. I was leaving and this time I wasn't coming back.

I passed the window and an unusual movement caught my eye. A woman, dressed in a dark brown, calf-length coat was running, waving her arms. As she came closer, I could see she was elderly, white-haired and familiar. She was staggering, out of breath, terrified. Then I saw why. A huge black dog bounded into view, chasing her. He was almost on her. Her mouth opened in a scream I couldn't hear.

Without thinking, I raced out of the room and out of the house, along the river path. No one else was around apart from a man in the distance, walking away. I saw a hunched bundle lying on the path ahead of me a few yards from the tree. There was no sign of the dog. Panting, I reached her and bent down. She had collapsed and was facing away from me. I touched her shoulder and she rolled over. I screamed and backed off. The dead eyes of Kathleen Lloyd stared straight at me, milky, the irises rolled up almost out of sight, her mouth open in a near-perfect O, her fingers clawed at her throat where blood coagulated.

Heavy footsteps thudded down the path toward me. The man had heard me. He was already fishing in his pocket and by the time he reached me, he was pressing numbers on his phone.

———

"There was nothing you could have done, Mrs. Chambers." The young policewoman handed me a cup of coffee in my kitchen. "Mrs. Lloyd was a very old lady. You heard the paramedics. They're pretty certain she had a heart attack. Shame though. There she was taking some exercise, doing all the things she should do to keep fit and healthy and this happens."

I stared at the dark-haired officer. She couldn't have been more than her early twenties. "You saw her face," I said. "She was terrified when she died. And I know why."

Oh, let her think I was a lunatic. She probably did anyway. She was a community police officer. She'd have heard the rumors about the crazy niece of Miss Grant's living all on her own in that vast, scary house.

The young woman smiled in what I'm sure she thought was a reassuring fashion. It made me want to slap her. My emotions and nerves were raw enough without some smart-arse child cop telling me she knew better!

"I asked the paramedic about that expression on her face. It was pretty unnerving, wasn't it? That and the blood on her throat. He said, she probably couldn't get her breath. You know, when the heart attack struck."

I struggled to keep my voice calm. "And what about the black dog."

"What dog?"

"I told you. I saw a big, black dog chasing her. That's why she was running. That's why she was terrified and that's why she had the heart attack. Has anyone found the dog yet? It needs to be put down. There's something seriously wrong with it."

The woman shrugged her shoulders and I gripped the edge of the table. One more smart comment and I wouldn't be able to restrain myself.

"No one else has seen a dog. Mr. Hawks, who called us, said he hadn't seen any dogs down there today. He remarked on how unusual that was."

"Perhaps something kept them away," I said.

The door opened and an older—male—police officer poked his head around. "If you're ready, Lynn, we're done here."

"I'll be right there." The policewoman stood up and took my empty coffee mug to the sink. "Will you be all right on your own, Mrs. Chambers? Is there anyone I can call to come and sit with you?"

I managed a smile. More of relief that she was going than for any other reason. "I'll be fine. Thank you."

She gave me a bemused look that only lacked the single cocked eyebrow to achieve full irony. "Well, if you're sure. Goodbye then. You really couldn't have done anything more. Take care of yourself and try not to dwell on today. It was her time, that's all."

I let them see themselves out. The front door slammed.

Above me, on the second floor, the gramophone started up again. Glenn Miller and His Orchestra and my aunt's voice singing along to her favorite song. Once again a whisper sounded in my ear.

"She's playing the devil's serenade."

I raced up to my bedroom and grabbed the suitcase, trying my damnedest to ignore the whispering echoes all around me and that music. That bloody song that sent terror shooting through every cell of my body and made me want to scream until I had no voice left. I forced myself to be governed by one thought alone—to get out of this house once and for all. Alive.

Chapter Eleven

I stayed in the same hotel as before, booking myself in for an initial two weeks. The first thing I did was see an estate agent and put the house on the market, carefully avoiding the need to go back there myself.

The hardest part was breaking the news to Shona.

"I'm so sorry it means you'll probably lose your rehearsal room, but I expect it'll take an age to sell the place anyway. Hopefully you'll be able to find somewhere else in the meantime."

We were sitting in Shona's cramped study at the former vicarage. Ancient books struggled to maintain their precarious foothold in bookcases designed for half the number of volumes they were expected to accommodate. Her desk was strewn with papers, and the windowsill groaned under the weight of potted plants.

Shona patted my hand. "The important thing is that you're all right. Where will you go, when the house is sold?"

I shrugged my shoulders. Truth to tell, I hadn't a clue. "I might go back to Chester." But as I said it I knew I never would. Nothing would make me want to go back to living in the same city as Neil.

"You could stay in this town," Shona said. "You'd be very welcome."

"Would I?"

"Of course you would. Why would you think otherwise?"

"Because of people in the town who remember my aunt. And all those crazy rumors." I thought of poor, dead Mrs. Lloyd. Shona must have read my mind.

"I spoke to Kathleen a couple of days ago. She remembered Nathaniel Hargest from when she was a girl. She also remembered your aunt and how shocked her mother was when she moved in with the old man. Most of what she knew came from her mother and grandmother. It's all superstition and innuendo, Maddie. Don't pay any attention to it."

"You didn't see her face, Shona." I shuddered. "She looked as if she'd died staring at a vision of hell itself." Shona said nothing. Before I could stop myself, I said, "I saw him." I told her about the impossible wind and the figure I'd seen. When I told her how the man I now knew to be Hargest had vanished, her expression changed. She looked concerned in a way I felt certain I wasn't going to like.

"Have you thought about seeing a doctor?"

That put me on the defensive. "Why would I? I'm not ill."

"But sometimes our minds can play tricks on us and—"

"I'm *not* sick, Shona. I thought you at least might believe me. I saw this inexplicable wind buffet that tree; its branches bent in ways they shouldn't be capable of. For heaven's sake, it blew me over. And I saw Nathaniel Hargest, as clearly as I saw Veronica, and Thelma as well. I don't have an explanation for it, but I know what I saw and it's frightening the life out of me."

Shona stared at me for a few moments, then licked her lips. "I'm sorry you had such a terrible fright, seeing Kathleen like that. It's never easy, finding a body. It's happened to me. But she died of a heart attack. The expression you saw was probably pain, shock even. It was all quite sudden and, even though she was eighty-eight, it was unexpected. Still she did have a long life."

Shona's words were delivered in a matter-of-fact tone. Well, why shouldn't they be? After all, as she'd told me, they weren't exactly best friends. But her attitude seemed almost callous. Dismissive. Not like the Shona I had grown to like.

I left soon after.

Charlie phoned and proved impossible to resist. "Look, why don't I do the jobs anyway? At the moment, the lack of sockets will be one more thing a potential buyer would have to put right. And, while I'm at it, why don't I put in the extra radiators on the top floors? Your buyers won't die of frostbite when they're being shown around."

What he said made sense. "Okay, go ahead. I'll meet you at the house and give you a spare set of keys so you can let yourself in and out."

"So you won't be there?"

"No, I've decided to stay elsewhere until it's sold."

"Oh, that's a shame."

I could tell he was waiting for an explanation, but I wasn't prepared to share with Charlie what I'd told Shona, especially not after her latest reaction.

Charlie and I arrived at the house at the same time and I was grateful for that. At least I didn't have to go in there alone and I'd forgotten to pack so many personal things I wanted to keep with me.

"Moving back in?" Charlie nodded to the suitcase in my hand.

"Oh no, I'm collecting some more of my things." I tried to appear nonchalant, but my heart was beating far too fast. I told myself nothing would happen while Charlie was there. I unlocked the door and handed him the spare keys.

I dropped the suitcase at the sight that met my eyes. "What the…?"

"You've had a break in." Charlie strode through the devastated hall into the kitchen. I stared at the upended table and dead leaves strewn all over the floor. It looked like a tornado had whirled through here, leaving devastation and ruin behind it.

"Oh my God!" Charlie's exclamation set me racing after him.

I stopped at the entrance. The cellar door was open. Tree roots, clinging together to form one giant mass, seemed to have forced their way through and now trailed across the floor. I looked down and screamed, "Charlie. Your foot!"

He pulled back, shaking off the root that had curled around it. His face was as white as mine must have been.

"What the hell can I do?" My voice cracked. "What *is* this?"

Charlie shook his head. "Pray," he said. "And get out of here. Never look back. Okay? Just get out of here."

But there was something I must take with me. My personal documents. I had a concertina file in the living room containing my birth certificate and every other valuable document I possessed.

I left Charlie staring down at the roots in the kitchen. As I tore across the hall, another barrier lifted partially in my brain. An image. A memory of Aunt Charlotte chanting. On the second floor. In the room that was now littered with broken furniture. She had stood at the window, holding my hand. I didn't understand her words, but when she had finished, she had squeezed my hand.

"It's going to be all right, Maddie. You're under their protection now. They'll keep you safe from harm."

I grabbed the concertina file and struggled to remember more, but nothing came.

I heard a yell. A man's cry of pain. Charlie.

I ran back to the kitchen. And disbelief.

The roots had disappeared. The cellar door was closed. I turned back to the hall. In those few seconds, the leaves had gone, the vases were back on their tables. Everything once again as it should be. I stared, incredulous at the neat and tidy hall. This was madness. I *couldn't* have imagined it all. And where was Charlie?

I called his name. I shouted up the stairs. I went back to the kitchen, picturing him lying at the foot of the cellar steps, injured and in pain, or unconscious and bleeding to death. Or worse. Maybe I was already too late. I couldn't leave him there. I would have to open the cellar door.

The smell of damp earth and rotting vegetation hit me the moment I cracked the door an inch.

No roots met me. I took a couple of nervous steps. "Charlie?"

My voice echoed around the bare walls. I listened. Not a sound. Switching the lights on revealed nothing out of the ordinary. Nothing to indicate the sight that had greeted us when we first arrived.

I wanted to run away, but I couldn't do that to Charlie. In that split second I realized he had come to mean more to me than merely an electrician I'd employed.

"Charlie?" I reached the bottom of the stairs and took a deep breath, I grabbed the flashlight and turned toward the corner where the roots grew. I shone the light at the clump of roots. They seemed even more luxuriant and appeared to have edged a little farther along the floor, but only an inch or two, if that. So what the hell had we seen in the kitchen?

I peered all round, shone the flashlight as best I could into dark places even the improved lighting couldn't penetrate. I couldn't bring myself to touch the roots, but they definitely did seem thicker and more serpentine.

Unless Charlie had gone upstairs, he must have left already. Maybe he saw something that scared him so much he fled.

But I would have heard him. Or the door opening at least.

Upstairs in the kitchen, I checked the back door. Locked and bolted. I went out the front. His van was still parked next to my car. He wasn't in the driver's seat. I looked around. No sign. I called his name. No response. He must still be in the house.

Reluctantly, I turned back and started up the stairs.

The giggling started almost immediately. I heard a hissing, "Hush!" It sounded like an older female. The childish laughter stopped. I swallowed. I would have given anything to be able to turn around and race back down the stairs, but Charlie must be up here. Maybe injured and in pain. If something happened to him, it would be all my fault. If he were found dead and he had been alive when I ran away, I would have that on my conscience for the rest of my life. No, I had to face this fear.

I gripped the stair rail with clammy hands and pushed on. As I reached the first landing, I thought I heard footsteps running along the corridor above. I told myself it was my imagination. My feet were lumps of concrete. They didn't want to move and I didn't want to move them, but I had to. Up another flight.

Whispering. Two children whispering to each other. I couldn't make out the words. In a way I was glad. Maybe I really didn't want to hear what they were saying. Plotting.

I made it to the next floor and clung on to the banister, too scared to let go. Terrified to look around and see what had been running along the corridor or who had been giggling. I forced my head to turn and look to the right. The rehearsal room door stood ajar.

I crept toward it and listened. Nothing. I pushed it open with one finger and stepped over the threshold.

There was nothing unusual. I saw the customary layout of chairs and tables left by the cast after their latest rehearsal. Now Shona had a key, they could come and go as they pleased. Evidently none of them had been bothered by whatever lurked in the shadows here. No, *I* was their only target.

Once I'd left the room, I took a deep breath. My stomach clenched. I would have to go into the junk room.

The door was closed. I hesitated. Maybe I should call out, but I didn't want to reveal my presence. Besides if Charlie was unconscious, who would answer? That's what really scared me.

I turned the door handle. A chill hit me in the face, with such a force it almost knocked me over. Inside, the already jumbled and broken furniture looked as if someone had attacked it with a sledgehammer. Shattered chairs, tables, shards of glass from ruined mirrors, littered the floor. Cupboards had been stacked up so that I couldn't see the back of the room clearly. Charlie could be in amongst this and I wouldn't know. Not unless I went in properly and worked my way through to the back.

Anxious to avoid tripping, I stepped carefully. Some of the debris could provide a deadly weapon to anyone with murder on their mind. Anyone—or anything.

I threw broken chair arms and legs out of the way and heard a crunch of glass under my feet. I looked down and picked up a small silver frame, carefully wiped it and stared at the image. Nathaniel Hargest glared back at me from the photograph I had seen in the picture of my aunt downstairs in the album.

I took in the thin, cruel lips and cold, hard eyes, the walking stick—topped by a silver lion—that he held in one hand. Could Aunt Charlotte really have surrendered herself to a man like this? It was hard to believe. Yet I had read the evidence written in her own hand. She had said she *had* to share his bed, but I still didn't have a clue why.

The giggling started again. It was coming from the doorway. I looked up.

This time, she made no attempt to run away. Veronica stared at me, her thumb in her mouth. We gazed at each other. She removed her thumb and began to hum.

"Serenade in Blue".

I stared at her. She stopped and her childish voice rang out. "It's his song. In this house, that's the devil's serenade."

Charlotte

Chapter Twelve

Midsummer Night 1964

Charlotte Grant set down her pen and closed her *Book of Shadows*. She stared out of the window. In the day's last fading light, she could still make out the shadow of the willow tree. Willow, such a force for good and Charlotte had long been fascinated by the ancient wisdom surrounding it. She'd made a study of it these past few years, since moving to this house. She knew her employer practiced dark arts, but she shut her mind to it—and sometimes her ears.

How many times had she resolved to leave? Too many to count, but where would she go? Not to her sister's. Marjorie didn't even know how low she'd sunk after Freddie's death. When the war ended, Charlotte left home and moved to London, but she couldn't find work. Eventually, dispirited and still grieving, she stopped trying. Marjorie knew nothing about this time in her life or about the shoplifting when she was penniless. She never knew about the arrest and how a strange man Charlotte had never met had made the charges go away. Nathaniel Hargest. She had been grateful, and both relieved and happy to agree to be his housekeeper. At least she would have a roof over her head.

It wasn't long before Charlotte began to realize that the gift of a new life her benefactor had given her was never going to be straightforward. She knew that the cries she sometimes heard at night and the strange thumps and crashes overhead as she lay in her bed were not merely evidence of Mr. Hargest's sexual proclivities. She pulled the blanket over her head when she heard a woman scream on the top floor, locked her door every night, and Mr. Hargest never came near her. She still didn't know how he had heard of her, or why he had saved her from an almost certain prison sentence.

Charlotte never ventured up to the top floor. Mr. Hargest said it wasn't necessary for her—or any of the constant stream of maids—to do so. Except those who disappeared of course. She never saw them again, quietly replaced them, and avoided the prying eyes and whispered conversations as she went about her business in the town.

If Charlotte closed her mind to the darkness that pervaded the top floor, she could stay here, fed and clothed. If she left she would be homeless again, with no references and no hope of finding another position before hunger and desperation took over once more. So Charlotte ignored the rumors of missing children, the sounds of chanting wafting into the house on previous Midsummer Nights when she had lain awake, clutching her talisman—a Green Man on a leather necklace that Freddie had given her, which she always wore under her clothes.

When it all got too much for her, she went down to the willow tree, stroked the ancient bark, listened to the whispering of the leaves and imagined the spirits that dwelt within it. Her fingers tingled with the power that flowed from its core, through her veins.

Spirits of willow protect me. Spirits of willow come to me. Spirits of willow let no harm reach me from the darkness and the evil ones...

This Midsummer Night was different. Tonight it was happening. Somehow she had always known it would and that one day Mr. Hargest would take her.

Charlotte turned from the window, smoothed down her long black gown and reached for the cloak given to her by Mr. Hargest. Her heart pounded uncomfortably. Her fingers shook as she struggled with the clasp at the neck. Panic rose from the pit of her stomach. Tonight. It would be tonight. Mr. Hargest had said so. Down by the tree, the coven would meet. Charlotte stared at her reflection as if the terrified, white-faced woman was some stranger she had never seen before. Her brown eyes blinked with rapid-fire speed. Tears threatened to well up, but she mustn't let that happen. Mr. Hargest would be angry with her, and the Lord and his Lady knew she didn't want to make him angry.

She pulled the sleeve of her gown down to her wrist, covering the darkening bruises where her employer had gripped her hard. Her neck still ached from when he had shaken her and broken the leather necklace so that her talisman fell to the floor. It had been her own fault. She had dared to say "no" when he first told her what plans he had for her.

"I will have a son and you will be its mother," he said. "You have been chosen. It is your destiny."

Charlotte had stared at him, unable to believe what she was hearing. In the nine years she had been Mr. Hargest's housekeeper, he had never laid a finger on her, either in anger or lust. He had shouted, sworn, thrown objects to hand when he lost his temper, but never any suggestion of anything improper. Recently things had changed. She had caught him looking at her differently when he didn't know she was watching. A lasciviousness had crept into his glances. Now he had revealed his true purpose. Tonight, at the Midsummer Feast, he would summon the darkness, aided by the faithful coven.

The door opened. Charlotte caught her breath and whirled round. Nathaniel Hargest stood, framed in the doorway, his unfashionable top hat and black coat sacrificed for a long cloak of black with gold thread picking out strange symbols that looked Egyptian but could have emanated from a far older civilization.

Tonight, Mr. Hargest gave barely a hint of his ninety-five years. He stood ramrod straight, over six feet tall, towering over Charlotte. A tall crown fashioned from bent twigs and painted gold added to his height and Charlotte shuddered when she realized that underneath the enveloping cloak, her employer was stark naked.

The dim light of the single table lamp in her room protected her from seeing what lay underneath that cloak, but the protrusion at the front of it left her in no doubt that he was aroused.

He passed his tongue slowly over his lips as if savoring a particularly delicious taste.

"Come, my dear. It is time to meet the others."

Charlotte shrank back. Her employer's expression darkened. He half turned and summoned two women who had been standing out of sight. They were naked. One young, the other middle-aged. They had the look of each other as a mother and daughter would. Neither spoke as they advanced toward Charlotte who couldn't move her feet. Fear tore at every pore of her body as each woman took one of her arms and propelled her forward. She staggered.

"Come, Charlotte." There was irritation in that voice. Another moment and he would become angry. The sooner she acquiesced to the inevitable, the sooner it would be over and if she didn't incur his wrath, she might make it out of there alive.

But he didn't want her dead, did he? Mr. Hargest had made it perfectly clear what he wanted. What he intended to get—by one means or another.

The two women silently led the quivering Charlotte down the stairs and out into the balmy night. In the distance, the church clock chimed the half hour. Eleven thirty. In half an hour the serious business of the night would begin. Charlotte tried to swallow but her mouth was too dry. A few yards away, a silent group of ten men and women stood, naked, each holding a candle. They had gathered a few yards from that strangely deformed willow tree, as if to mock its goodness with their evil. Leaves rustled in the slight breeze. It knew they were there. It knew the man's dark design. As Charlotte was thrust into the middle of the circle, the assembled started a low chant that seemed to find an echo in the ground beneath, which trembled under Charlotte's feet.

Hargest took up his position opposite her. Now her eyes were accustomed to the gloom and the flickering candlelight, Charlotte made out a low black table toward which her two guards pushed her. No one looked directly at her or at Hargest. All stood with heads bowed as if in the presence of some great deity.

Hargest raised his arms, letting the cloak fall away to reveal his naked body. The quavering light illuminated the wrinkled skin and white chest hair. Charlotte looked away. She didn't want to see what else it illuminated.

The two acolytes removed her cloak and pushed her still closer toward the table. Charlotte fought against their grasp, but her employer had chosen these two well. They were strong. Maybe farm workers. So far, she hadn't recognized one person among those gathered there.

The women forced her onto the table. Escape was impossible. The coven had moved closer and clustered together on three sides, leaving one side free for their master.

Charlotte closed her eyes. Firm hands grasped her ankles and wrists and dragged her legs apart. Someone took hold of the hem of her gown and tore it from her body. The rush of air to her naked flesh made her cry out. She didn't even think of the shame of lying there, her body exposed to this group of strangers. At that moment, all she cared about was getting out of there alive and unhurt. She bit her lip until she tasted blood, squeezed her eyes tight shut and tried to will herself away from the scene of her certain violation.

The chanting began again—a strange, foreign language that sounded nothing like any she had heard before. As ancient as the symbols on Hargest's cloak perhaps. Cold hands probed between her legs. The chanting grew more urgent. Behind her the branches of the ancient tree creaked.

At the first stab of her pain, cries of ecstasy issued from the coven. At the age of thirty-seven, Charlotte was no longer a virgin.

Someone was forcing his way into her. Stretching her wide. Tearing her. A loud grunt filled her ears and hot, sour breath made her retch. Charlotte opened her eyes and screamed.

Hargest was on top of her. Barely human. His eyes—flaming red pools of fire. Windows to the gates of hell itself. He grunted again, thrusting himself still further into her unwilling body. Shards of pain tore at her insides. She tossed her head from side to side and struggled against the firm hands holding her down. She tried to kick out, but her captors were too strong for her.

The creature that was part Hargest and part demon opened its mouth. Fangs filled the gaping maw. Its tongue snaked out and licked her cheek, burning it with stinging, hellish saliva.

Another agonizing stab of pain tore through her. "No!" But Charlotte heard her cry from far away, as soft hands embraced her spirit and guided it toward the tree.

"You will be safe with us. Trust us."

Healing warmth flooded her consciousness.

"Where am I?"

"You are here with us. Safe within the tree."

"But the tree is his. This is his land."

"He has taken the darkness from the tree. We are the light he cannot reach."

"I don't understand. I can't see you. I can't see anything."

"Rest now. Rest and sleep…"

Charlotte awoke with a start. For a couple of seconds she forgot about last night. Then the pain struck. Knives of agony scythed through her insides and between her legs. She lay in her bed, clothed in one of her ankle length cotton nightgowns. She struggled to sit up, but fresh torments made her gasp and lie back, panting.

The sun filtered through the drapes. She peered at the clock on the bedside table. Just after eight. Normally she was up by seven. Her brain felt sluggish, shrouded by some awful memory that she was about to recall and when she did, the fear began. But her bladder was full. She would have to get up somehow.

She pushed back the sheet and tried to move her legs. Every movement sent fresh waves of pain coursing through her. She fought against the urge to give up. It wasn't an option. She had to get to the bathroom. Somehow she got to her feet and the room swayed. She steadied herself by holding on to one of the four bedposts and waited for the worst to subside. Finally, she trusted herself to take a tentative step. Then another and another. Achingly slowly, she made her way out of the bedroom and down the corridor. The house was silent, although by now the cook and her maid would have arrived and be preparing breakfast.

In the bathroom, Charlotte pulled her nightdress over her head and winced at the purple, red, blue, and black bruises that seemed to cover most of her exposed body.

She whimpered with the burning, stinging pain as she relieved herself. Then she ran a bath, sinking gratefully into the hot, soothing water.

Last night's memories gradually returned, each more unreal that the last. The horror of her violation at the hands of Nathaniel Hargest and whatever…thing…he had summoned up from the depths of hell. Then the spirits that had rescued her, taken her from her body and transported her somehow into the tree itself. But that wasn't possible. None of this was possible.

When Charlotte returned to her bedroom, she took her suitcase down and began to pack. She had got no further than emptying her wardrobe when the door flew open.

Charlotte gasped. Her employer, dressed once more in his familiar black Edwardian morning suit, strode in. A half-smile changed into a frown in a second.

"Oh no, Charlotte. You will not be leaving this house. You will never leave this house."

"You can't force me to stay here. I'm not your prisoner." Charlotte had no idea how those words dared to issue from her mouth. He would make her pay for that.

Nathaniel Hargest stared at her. "In nine months you will bear my child. A child who is destined for greatness. I say you cannot leave this house and indeed you will not. You will live here until the day you die. You belong here."

Charlotte stared at him, the impact of his words barely registering. How could he know she was pregnant? It was too soon even for her to know, but somewhere deep inside her mind, she knew he was right. He, or that demon, had planted his seed in her last night. But what sort of child would she bear? Hargest closed the door behind him and she sank onto the bed, for once oblivious to the pain of her injuries. In nine months, would she birth a son…or a monster?

Chapter Thirteen

Charlotte moved heavily in her last month of pregnancy. Her ankles had swollen and her legs throbbed painfully. Even the effort of rising from her bedroom chair and inching her way over to the desk under the window made her grit her teeth and support her distended belly. By the time she reached her destination, her dwindling energy reserves were exhausted. She sank down gratefully onto the stool and opened the drawer. She pulled out a black, leather-bound book and her fingers traced the gold embossed lettering of her *Book of Shadows*. Charlotte turned the pages and came across her last entry, written days before Midsummer Night:

Now he tells me I must share his bed.

But that hadn't been his purpose. His purpose had been to use her, ritually impregnate her and, after the baby was born…

Not for the first time, cold fear struck Charlotte. Was her sole purpose to be the bearer of Nathaniel Hargest's heir? What use would he have for her after the baby was weaned? He'd already told her she couldn't leave the house. Not until the day she died. What if that day was to arrive sooner than later?

Charlotte rummaged further in her drawer and pulled out her diary. It had been a while since she had written in it. She found a new blank page, selected a pen from her desk and wrote the date. March 7th, 1965.

I am sick at heart today. The baby kicks me unmercifully day and night. I feel it isn't prepared to wait until the proper time. God help me, I don't want this child. I want nothing of Mr. Hargest's. I must get away somehow after this baby is born, or I am sure he will kill me. Yet he confuses me. When he is angry and his eyes darken, I swear I can see again that demon that raped me. Yet, on other occasions, he can be strangely attentive. I have never seen this side of him before. Except perhaps when he asks me to play "Serenade in Blue". I wish he didn't like it so much. That is OUR song—mine and Freddie's. He sullies it by even listening to it. But I will not let him spoil it for me. I will not let it become a devil's serenade. His serenade.

I had a little more energy yesterday afternoon. The sun shone on a beautiful spring-like day and I made my way to the willow tree. Only there can I find peace, despite what happened close by. The good spirits of the tree comforted me as I sat on the branch. I was frightened of them at first. How strange that seems now. They are my friends. They will protect me. It almost makes staying here worth it, if I can be near them. They bring me such solace and comfort. Of course, I am the only one who can see them, and it is a public right of way, so I shall have to be more careful to notice who is around when I speak to them. Yesterday, Mrs. Price from the shop caught me, apparently talking to myself. She gave me a strange look and pulled her dog away from me.

A knife-like pain shot through Charlotte and she dropped the pen. She felt wetness between her legs and struggled to her feet as another agony struck her.

The baby. But it was too soon.

Charlotte half crawled to her door. Mercifully, Lily—the agency maid—was taking towels to the bathrooms. Seeing Charlotte in obvious distress, she dropped them and rushed to help her.

"Oh, Miss Grant. Whatever is it? Is the baby coming?"

Charlotte nodded, her breath coming in gasps.

"I'll call an ambulance. Let's get you back to bed." Charlotte leaned gratefully on her as the young woman steered her. She was stopped by a voice that boomed along the hall.

"There will be no need for an ambulance. I have made arrangements. Take her back to bed. I shall call my doctor."

The labor pains were so intense and frequent, Charlotte had no energy to protest. Lily hesitated but did as she was told.

"There we are. Nothing wrong with a home birth," she said. "I was born at home. The midwife delivered me. My mum always said it was better at home. Too many germs in hospital. You never know what you might catch. Go in having a baby and come out with some deadly tropical disease that no one's found a cure for. Besides which," she said as she tucked Charlotte back into bed, "there's less prying eyes and gossiping tongues at home, isn't there?"

Charlotte blinked at her. The last thing she needed reminding of at this moment was her unmarried, disgraced state. Lily bit her lip.

"Shall I fluff your pillows a bit, Miss Grant?"

"I'm fine, thank you, Lily." Charlotte didn't bother to conceal the edge in her voice. She was in too much pain to care about the blundering girl's finer feelings. And she was scared. Pray God, the doctor was a real one and not one of Mr. Hargest's coven.

"I'm Dr. Faulkner and this is my assistant, Nurse Ray." Through her pain, Charlotte became aware of a young doctor with ginger hair and a pleasant smile. Standing next to him was a middle-aged woman with short, permed, graying hair, and an equally friendly expression.

A wave of relief flowed through Charlotte's brain. They seemed perfectly normal, qualified medical professionals. Hargest did not accompany them.

"You're quite far along," the doctor said, "but the baby is a little premature, so he or she may be a tad small and could need a tiny bit of help, but you'll soon be greeting your new little one. So, hold tight and let's get this baby born."

Dr. Faulkner disappeared from sight. Nurse Ray took Charlotte's hand as more pain struck with tidal force.

"Now," Dr. Faulkner said, "push! This one's in a great hurry. I can see the head. Push!"

Charlotte strained and screamed as she pushed with every ounce of strength she could summon. Minutes ticked by. Still the commands to push. When she had no more strength left, she still found some. The baby must be born. One final surge.

"That's it! You've done it." Dr. Faulkner came into view briefly. He grinned and his eyes sparkled. "You have a very handsome baby boy."

Nurse Ray rescued her hand from Charlotte's fierce grasp and a few seconds later, Charlotte's baby let out his first protesting wail.

Relief turned to fear in a second. "Is he?" Charlotte could hardly bring herself to ask the question that had plagued her all the months she had carried him. "Is he…?"

Dr. Faulkner laid a hand on her arm. "Nurse Ray is wrapping him up in a blanket. He's a good weight and you have a beautiful, healthy baby. Didn't need any help at all. And he has a healthy pair of lungs in him."

The nurse came into view. She held a soft white blanket with a squirming bundle and a broad smile lit up her face. "Here's your baby, Mrs. Grant."

Charlotte resisted the temptation to correct the nurse. All that mattered was that this baby was whole and healthy and betrayed none of the origins of his conception.

She held out her arms for him and the nurse laid him carefully down. Charlotte took a deep breath and looked down at a pair of blue eyes and a chubby pink face. Tiny hands with perfectly formed nails paddled the air. Gently, she pulled the blanket aside and saw the perfect limbs and torso. The child kicked, screwed his face up and began to bawl. From not wanting him, Charlotte's emotions sea-changed and she was filled with a fierce, protective love for this helpless infant she had brought into the world.

No one is going to harm you. Not while I have breath in my body.

"Your milk will come through soon," the nurse said. "Then you can feed baby."

Voices spoke outside the room. The door opened and Hargest advanced toward the bed. A half smile played at his lips. His collar length white hair was neatly combed as always, and in his ever-immaculate morning suit and pristine white, stiff collar, he didn't present the picture of a father who had been anxiously pacing the corridor.

He peered over at the baby, with scarcely a glance at the mother.

"Everything went extremely well, Mr. Hargest," Dr. Faulkner said.

"Yes, so I can see. And I am sure I can rely on your discretion."

"Absolutely. And Nurse Ray as well."

"Good. Good."

In Charlotte's arms, the baby had quieted down and seemed to have drifted off to sleep. Once again Hargest peered down at him and Charlotte got a whiff of the expensive cigars her employer smoked. This time, as he straightened up, a smile creased his wrinkled features. "You have done well, Charlotte. As I knew you would."

The kindness in his tone startled her. How could this man—so capable of extreme violence against her—show such gentleness? But, she reminded herself, even Hitler loved his dogs.

The days that followed only served to bring Charlotte closer to her son. She knew love she had never dreamed of. Yet, ten days after he was born, the child still had no name. Charlotte dared to raise the subject at breakfast.

"I must register his birth," she said as Hargest ate his toast. She poured him more coffee.

"I will take care of that in due course." There was an edge to his voice that sent a warning to Charlotte to tread carefully.

"I could go into Rokesby Green and save you the job."

Nathaniel Hargest flung down the last morsel of toast onto his plate, wiped his hand on his napkin and threw his chair back. "I said there is no need. As there was no need to leave this house to buy that damned rocking horse. You are to stay here and look after the child until I decide his future."

"His future? But his future is with me."

"No, Charlotte. This boy is special. He is destined to serve the master. When he is five years old, he will be initiated. Until that time, he will live where I say he lives. He has much to learn."

"No!" Charlotte's cry came from the pit of her stomach. She doubled over, clutching her stomach.

Across the room, Hargest's eyes shone red. "Don't dare to defy me, Charlotte. You are the child's mother and deserving of my respect. I allow you to live here in some comfort and that is my gift. I can remove it whenever I want. Don't forget that. Get out of my sight and attend to my son. I hear him crying again."

Charlotte fled the room for the sanctity of the nursery. This was what she had most feared. Hargest would groom her son into the same kind of monster he was. That couldn't be allowed to happen. Somehow she had to stop it.

Her son was asleep when she crept out of the room and closed the door.

The next morning, the nursery was empty.

Chapter Fourteen

Charlotte stared. The cot was gone, along with her son and almost every trace of him. Only the antique rocking horse she had brought home so proudly. It stood in a corner, in need of a fresh coat of paint, but otherwise in perfect working order.

Anger spewed out from Charlotte, along with her tears. Physical pain racked her body. The terrible wrench of losing her baby. She quit the room and fled downstairs. In the kitchen she sped past the startled cook, into the scullery where she found what she was looking for. A mallet.

Leaving the cook staring after her, Charlotte hurried back to the nursery and straight to the rocking horse. She raised the mallet and brought it down hard on the wooden toy. The sound of splintering wood spurred her on to do more damage. She stopped when the thing toppled over, one of its rockers completely shattered and the rest of it looking sorry and beaten.

With a cry of animal pain, Charlotte thrust the mallet away from her. It skidded across the wooden floor and crashed against the skirting board.

She sank to her knees and let out her suffering. Great heaving sobs that tore from the depths of her soul and seemed never to end. For three hours, her tears poured out, dried up, only to be refreshed and flow again. Her throat ached and burned from the strain of her sobs.

No one came.

The house was hushed. Whether Hargest was home or on his foul business, she knew not and cared less. He had taken her son, as he said he could, and given him to strangers. He might as well have ended her own life there and then.

It was early afternoon when Charlotte emerged from the empty nursery. Disoriented and unsteady, she staggered to her bedroom and once again reached for her suitcase. This time no one came to stop her.

She filled it with her best clothes, her *Book of Shadows*, and her diary, locked it and heaved it off the bed. Five minutes later, she opened the front door to a blast of warm spring air.

She hesitated. Once again she thought of her sister. Newly married Marjorie, who didn't even know Charlotte had been pregnant and certainly wouldn't approve, or want to be saddled with her in her nice new, semi-detached home.

Fleetingly Charlotte thought of the tree. If she could only give herself up to it. Become one with the tree spirits.

Crazy thoughts. No. Marjorie it would have to be. She didn't have to tell her everything. Just that Mr. Hargest had decided to dispense with her services. She could think of a good reason on her way there. Right now, she needed to catch a bus to the railway station four miles away.

With her back to the river, Charlotte began to walk up the gravel path leading to the main High Street. She got as far as the gate separating Hargest House's land from the public highway.

The tall figure wearing his familiar top hat barred her way. He seemed to have appeared from nowhere. Charlotte gave a cry and dropped her suitcase.

"Where is my son?" She surprised herself. All the fear she had felt for this man had vanished. All she cared about at that moment was her baby, but she had allowed herself to think only of her own escape. Guilt poured into her mind. She would never be so selfish again.

"My son is being cared for. You will not see him until you are needed again."

"And when is that?"

"When he is five years old. On the day you must present him to the master."

"Never!"

He gripped her arm tight and Charlotte flinched from the pain. "You will obey me or you will never see him again. I am making this concession to you. Take it, and this house and all that is in it will eventually be yours. Refuse and face the consequences."

Charlotte saw the red flame in his eyes. She didn't need to ask what the consequences would be.

Hargest pushed her back toward the house. Her suitcase remained where it had fallen.

Charlotte no longer cared about the contents or if she ever saw them again.

Days passed and Charlotte once again found solace in her diary. She sat at her desk, staring out of the window at the willow tree and the passersby, laughing, sometimes embracing, swinging children high up into the air, throwing balls and sticks for their dogs. They lived happy, normal lives. Each one of them had far more freedom than she had.

It had been Marjorie's birthday and Charlotte had toyed with the idea of pouring her heart out to her sister in a letter, but in the end decided against it. Marjorie had no concept of the supernatural. She would have merely been angry with Charlotte for becoming pregnant by her boss and, in any case, what could her sister do? Charlotte knew Hargest well enough to be certain he had hidden her son away where no one could find him. Even after this short time, the baby would have a new identity and would be brought up to recognize the destiny his father had mapped out for him.

Only by staying here would Charlotte have any chance of seeing him again—or even, by some miracle, getting him back. She had to hold on to that forlorn hope, however tenuous because it was all she had to live for. This monstrous deity Hargest worshiped valued the role of the mother enough to stop him from destroying her. He needed her, at least for the next few years. She would remain his virtual prisoner. So be it if it meant she would see her son again.

Months passed, the seasons changed, all slipping by virtually unnoticed by the woman who stared through her bedroom window, or went through the motions of keeping the house in order—the house that would, so she was told, be hers one day. Polishing silver and brassware kept her occupied, but nothing kept her mind off her one train of thought. Her son.

She never left Priory St. Michael these days, and her trips up to the shops were increasingly infrequent. Being the subject of hushed whispers, disapproving glances and hurriedly terminated conversations made her uncomfortable in the extreme. She preferred to spend her time tending her garden, planting, nurturing, and harvesting.

Another Midsummer Night brought another festival near the willow tree but, to her relief she was not required to attend. She spent the anniversary of the night she had conceived the little boy alone in her room, weeping softly.

The following day, she went down to the willow. Although it was warm, there was no one around. Some charred grass and ashes provided the only evidence of the previous night's revelries. Charlotte kicked a burnt twig with the toe of her shoe. The leafy branches of the willow provided a canopy as she sat on the long, low branch and gazed upward at the patchwork blue sky.

She leaned back against the gnarled, ancient trunk, and closed her eyes. Lulled by the warmth, she drifted, and the sounds of the river, the birds singing, and the leaves rustling faded into the background. A strange sensation of weightlessness overtook her and when she opened her eyes, she gasped at what she saw. All around her was dark except that when she turned her head, a streak of light shone through from far beyond.

Charlotte slowly stood, testing the invisible floor beneath her. She looked down but could only see blackness, without form or substance. Her feet rested on something that was both solid and nonexistent. She shrugged off the impossibility. Reason was for later. Now she had to find her way out. She made her way slowly toward the source of the light, putting out her hands in front of her and to the sides, hoping to touch some kind of wall, but finding none.

As she approached it, the light grew stronger, brighter, so that she had to blink and her eyes teared up. Instinctively, she raised her hand to her forehead, trying to shield herself from the harshness of the white light.

"Charlotte."

The call was little more than a whisper. Charlotte stopped and spun around, but behind her was the same blackness that was above her, beneath her and to the sides. She turned back.

"Who are you? Where am I? What is this place?"

"You are safe, Charlotte. Safe with us."

The tree spirits. She recognized their soft touch on her arms even if she still couldn't see them.

"Let us guide you."

The voice was behind her. Charlotte struggled to turn and face it.

"No. Our appearance will scare you. Walk forward. Let us help you."

The light seemed softer somehow. She didn't need her hand to shield her eyes anymore and it was being clasped gently behind her by something she wasn't allowed to see, yet Charlotte wasn't scared. Curiously, the granite block of grief she had felt these past months had lifted.

"You are here."

Her arms were free. The light was now slightly to one side of her. The blackness was gone. She looked around at the strange room, with its walls of brick and mortar. Strange woody veins ran through them. Charlotte stared, fascinated. She looked down at her feet. Beneath her lay a bed of willow leaves, soft and spring green. Their sweet sappy smell drifted up to her nostrils. She plucked up courage to look around, but there was no one there. The spirits must have retreated out of sight. It wouldn't have to be far. A few inches behind her was the familiar blackness.

In front of her, the wall was opaque, as if she was peering through a mist or a curtain of gauze. She reached out to touch it but her fingers found solid brick. It made no sense. She ran her hands down it, as she stood at arm's length. She moved closer, but still what she felt and what she saw remained at odds with each other. Impossibly so.

Through the haze, broken furniture, an old mattress, a kitchen stool with one leg missing, were all stacked in a corner of the room she recognized as the cellar of Hargest House.

"But this is impossible. I can't be…"

"Your eyes tell you it is possible. You are part of the house now. Only for a short while. Then you will return and all will be well. But you will understand and remember, when it is the right time."

"But my son. Where is my son? What has that evil monster done with him?"

"He is well and being cared for. He has a family."

"But they're devil worshipers."

"All will be well, Charlotte. Now you must return."

"I have so many questions." Tiredness overwhelmed her. When she awoke, she was still sitting on the branch, leaning against the tree. She glanced at her watch. She had apparently been out of it for no more than ten minutes. Charlotte looked around. No one to be seen. In the distance the faint thrum of traffic reached her as it moved up and down the High Street. She stood and stretched. With one backward glance at the tree, she made her way slowly back to the house, struggling in vain to remember the strange dream.

By the time she opened the door of Hargest House, she felt refreshed, as if all the horror of the past few months had been lifted.

From then on, whenever she thought of her son, it was with a new hope. Somehow she knew. All would be well.

Over the next two years, Nathanial Hargest kept himself to himself and Charlotte was barely aware of his comings and goings. He had no further use for her at present. He was civil to her on the occasions when their paths crossed, but there was no attempt at conversation, except where staff was concerned. These days, she was barely aware of any of his satanic rituals. He seemed to have disbanded the coven, since the night she had conceived her son. Maybe he had no further use for them. Midsummer had passed twice with no sight or sound of revelry—and Charlotte had waited by her bedroom window at midnight, looking out toward the tree, but it stood in deep darkness.

Charlotte's life had fallen into a dull routine of keeping house and supervising the continually changing roster of agency cooks and housemaids, none of whom lasted more than a few months at most before they fell foul of their employer's temper. If his meal was undercooked, overcooked, under-seasoned, over-seasoned, or merely not to his taste that day, the plate would be thrown and Charlotte would be summoned to dismiss the poor cook concerned. If he found a speck of dust, the maid would have to go. It was getting harder and harder to find anyone prepared to work at the house. Even the agencies themselves were becoming reluctant to supply anyone. Charlotte heard the catch in the voice on the other end of the phone when she gave her name.

Whenever she thought of her son, it was with sadness but always that indestructible belief that all would be well. All she had to do was hang on to that belief, and not question it, even though she still didn't even know his name.

On a stormy summer night, Charlotte sat up in bed. Her skin prickled. Something had woken her. Maybe a clap of thunder. She listened. A flash of lightning lit up her room. In the corner, a shape moved. Charlotte let out a cry and snapped on the bedside lamp. She clutched the sheet and blanket to her, every muscle in her body trembling. She stared at the corner of the room. There was nothing there. After a few minutes, she lay back down and closed her eyes, but the lamp remained on.

Just my imagination. There's nothing there. I couldn't have seen it. It was the lightning. Nothing else.

But part of her brain wouldn't let go the memory of that strange tree-like creature—with branches for arms—that watched her from the corner of her room.

Weeks drifted by until another night when she awoke from a sound sleep. This time she had fallen asleep reading. Her lamp was still switched on and her book lay on the floor where it had fallen. Maybe the noise of it landing there had woken her. Charlotte lay back down and took deep breaths to calm herself and her irrational fear.

A loud thump crashed overhead. Charlotte sprang out of bed. Another thump set her mantelpiece ornaments rattling.

She grabbed her robe and wrenched open her door. The corridor was silent and dark. She reached for the light switch and the bulbs flickered on.

Another thump. Louder now she was outside her room.

Only she and Mr. Hargest were in the house. His rooms were on the second floor, directly above hers. Maybe he had fallen out of bed. After all, he was a very old man. Her heart lifted at the thought. Maybe she would go up there and find him lying on the floor, the life extinguished from him.

The thought of the release that would bring spurred her on up the stairs. She paused on the landing. Silence. She flicked the light switch and the dark, gloomy corridor was bathed in welcome light. Charlotte started toward her employer's bedroom door. The noise of two more thumps stopped her. The sound was coming from the top floor—where she never ventured.

Charlotte hesitated. She could think of no reason why Mr. Hargest would be up there, but she had to find out.

Her heart beat loudly in her ears as she mounted the stairs. The thundering above her grew, intensified. The house itself pounded in rhythm with her heart. Charlotte crammed her hands against her ears, but, as she reached the top step, the vibration was all around her. The floor trembled beneath her feet. The walls pulsated with the sound. It echoed down the corridors either side of her. She turned from one to another and screamed as all the doors flew open at the same time. A ball of wind rushed at her, hitting her on her left side. The stench of sulfur filled her nostrils. Charlotte's knees buckled and she sank to the floor. A dark, cloaked figure appeared from the nearest room, a few feet away, untroubled by the wind that buffeted Charlotte as she crouched, unable to escape. Unable even to move. Terror sent a voice screaming through her mind.

I'm going to die.

The figure reached her, bent down and lifted her by her shoulders. Charlotte cried out as she recognized Nathaniel Hargest. His eyes blazed red flames. His mouth opened to reveal animal fangs. The wind and the noise stopped. For a second, the house went unnaturally quiet. As if waiting.

"Dear God, help me."

Charlotte's plea broke the silence with a narrow wail. The creature that Hargest had become roared. Charlotte closed her eyes. Surely he would kill her. But he dragged her to the room. The smell of sulfur was unbearable. Charlotte gagged. She vomited up the remains of her last meal and Hargest thrust her from him so that she skidded across the wooden floor, hitting her shoulder on the leg of a table laid out as an altar. In some strange way the pain came almost as a relief. At least she was still alive.

The pulsating heartbeat of the house resumed, quietly at first, then building. Charlotte drew herself into a tight ball. The sulfur fumes stifled her. She coughed. Her eyes streamed.

Hargest stood in front of her. His skin blackened, as if burned to charcoal. His arms hung at his sides, strangely branch-like. His head was gnarled and grotesquely distorted. His fang-filled mouth seemed to have receded as if he no longer needed it. Only his eyes blazed their unnatural red fire. Charlotte's fear locked her limbs in a catatonic paralysis.

A thunderous roar shook the house. At the far end of the room, a dark cloud swirled. Within it a shape moved. Still Charlotte couldn't move, although her mind screamed at her to get away. In front of her unblinking eyes, the shape grew. Earsplitting roars tore through her body. In the billowing charcoal cloud, a leonine creature threw back its unnatural head and opened its mouth. The fanfare of hell roared and spewed through the room. Instead of fur, blue-black scales covered its body. Vicious clawed feet raked the floor and its tail coiled like a serpent. Worse still, an erect and deadly phallus—culminating in a snake's head, with darting forked tongue. Mercifully, although the creature was only a few feet away, it didn't seem to see her.

Hargest bowed to it and the demon roared again. Charlotte's head pounded with the vibration. Her ears rang. Her eyes transfixed on that evil-looking phallus.

Dear Lord and Lady, take me now. Let me die now…

She managed to close her eyes and tried to will herself away from the room. She thought of the tree spirits, and then the smell of sulfur wasn't so strong.

In the distance, she heard Hargest speak. "My lord."

A hand touched her arm.

Charlotte fainted.

When Charlotte came to, the paralysis had gone and, although her limbs ached, she could move them. Pins and needles struck her painfully in her hands and feet. Behind her, the altar was a plain, wooden, discarded dining table once more. Apart from that, the room was empty. No sign of any hellish creature or Nathaniel Hargest. She could almost believe she had dreamed it all, except for the lingering smell of sulfur still polluting the atmosphere.

She glanced down at her soiled nightdress and became aware of another foul smell wafting up from her body. Her fear had loosened her bowels. Leaning on the table for support, Charlotte dragged herself to her feet and staggered out of there. An hour later, both she and the room were cleansed. A pale sun had risen above the horizon on a chilly autumnal morning. November 1st. Charlotte selected her warm winter coat and slipped out of the back door, where she met the cook arriving to prepare breakfast.

Charlotte cleared her throat. "I'm sorry, I don't know if Mr. Hargest is at home or not today. Assume he is and prepare breakfast for him anyway. I won't require anything and I'll be back shortly, but there's an urgent errand I must run."

The older woman looked as if she was about to ask a question. Charlotte was in no mood for answers and hurried away.

The river was swollen after the previous week's heavy rains. The willow tree had shed half its leaves in preparation for winter. A gentle breeze sent a shower of them floating down onto Charlotte's head and shoulders. She sat down on the branch, leaned against the trunk, closed her eyes and prayed for the tree spirits.

The soothing calmness of their presence flowed through her veins, warming and lulling her. Once again, she was in that place that couldn't exist. The other dimension that let her believe she could be in fabric of the house somehow. The quiet cellar emerged through its gauzy haze and she knew the spirits could hear her thoughts.

"He brought evil into the house. He was transformed."

"Yes, Charlotte. The evil one he brought is from a time beyond time as you know it. Before your prehistory. It is a forest demon. The most deadly of them all."

"But what does it have to do with Nathaniel Hargest? I don't understand. Is this the demon who will take my son?"

"There is a way to stop that, but it will take great courage. The demon's power is greater than even Hargest knows. He sold his soul to it to gain his wealth, but it is hungry for more and demands great sacrifice. We can save your son, Charlotte, but it will come at a price. The first is that you may never leave Hargest House."

"He told me that. He told me I may never leave, that the house will be mine and that I will present my son when he is five years old..." Charlotte's voice broke. Despite the comforting web laid around her by the tree spirits, despair scythed through her.

Soft tendrils stroked her face and, with a sudden shock, Charlotte realized they were twig-like, yet green, slender, pliable. Their healing powers soothed away the pain and calmed her once again.

The spirit spoke again. "Hargest will not live much longer and his soul is forfeit to the demon. He will do its bidding for the rest of eternity as its minion and slave. After he is dead, Hargest's spirit will return to this house to do his master's work but, when he does, you will be ready. You are under the protection of the Lord and Lady and he will not harm you. But, be assured, you must do as we advise you or the demon will destroy the protection we have created for you. It will be able to see you and if it sees you, it will come for you. If not you, then your son. Do you understand?"

"I understand."

"Be calm. Rest. All will be well."

Charlotte slept and, in her dreams, a tall slender lady in green and gold presented her with a willow wand.

When Charlotte awoke, still on the tree branch, the wand was in her hand.

Chapter Fifteen

The next couple of years passed and life settled into the closest approximation of normality possible in that house. Charlotte managed to tolerate her situation, fueled by her hatred for Nathaniel Hargest and her determination to get her son back. Every day brought her closer to his fifth birthday and the time she would see him again.

One night, she awoke suddenly. Above her, the floorboards creaked. Someone was moving around. Hargest. A door slammed.

In a second she was out of bed and at her door. The stairs to the top floor were uncarpeted and the sound of three sets of footsteps echoed in the distance. She grabbed her robe from the hook on the door and wrapped it around her. Careful not to make a sound, she slowly opened the door and peered out. Another door slammed. Farther away this time. Charlotte hesitated. Part of her wanted to dive back into bed and pull the sheet over her head. Another part needed to know what Hargest was up to. Who did the other footsteps belong to? She knew of no one in the house but her and her employer.

Barefoot, she made her way up the two flights of stairs. On the top landing, the lights blazed. She padded down the corridor to her left and listened at each door. She paused outside the third one. Scuffling. Furniture being dragged across the uncarpeted floor. She bent and peered through the keyhole. Someone moved. Not Hargest. A woman, in a long black gown or cloak.

Charlotte's heart beat faster. The lights in the corridor flickered and extinguished, plunging her into darkness. She froze. A pale red light pulsed through the door frame and the pounding began again. Then the roar. A woman's scream. A man's terrified cry.

Without thinking, Charlotte wrenched the door open and stared at the horrific scene. The man and the woman were laid flat on tables. Both were bound by their wrists and ankles. Hargest was dressed in the black and gold robe she had seen that Midsummer Night. He wielded a silver scimitar. Behind him, the swirling, foul black smoke, the glimpse of the scaly body and grotesque lion's head.

The terrified man caught Charlotte's eye and she recognized him. Dr. Faulkner. "Help us, please! Please!"

Hargest glared at Charlotte. She couldn't help herself. She backed off.

"Get away from here!" he roared.

The beast was almost fully manifested. Charlotte knew it mustn't see her. Hargest brought down the scimitar and blood gushed from the doctor's severed head. It rolled onto the floor. Charlotte screamed. The woman let out an anguished wail that seemed to rise from her very soul. Hargest raised his dripping scimitar once more. He lowered it and the woman fell silent. Her neck gushed blood as her head joined her companion's, its terrified dead eyes turned toward Charlotte. She screamed again. Nurse Ray was staring at her, mouth open in eternal, silent terror.

Charlotte raced downstairs, into her room, locked the door and cowered on the floor. She crammed her hands to her ears to block out the sounds from above. The roars, thumps and crashes that set the whole house shaking, and other, even more dreadful sounds of something being dragged down the stairs. The bodies. The innocent man and woman she had been powerless to even attempt to save. The house went quiet after the front door slammed, but still she didn't dare leave her room. Her tears flowed—great heaving sobs. She told herself she had been too late to save them. That if the demon had seen her, she would have been dead too. Or her son. Any action would have been in vain—and worse.

By morning, her tears had dried. Charlotte Grant washed and dressed herself, ready for the day. She ventured up to the top floor, expecting a scene of unspeakable carnage, but there was no trace that anything had happened. No blood. Just two bare tables and the lingering stench of sulfur. She opened the tall cupboard at the far end of the room. The foul smell was stronger here, but the cupboard was empty.

Charlotte shut the door tight, her mouth set in a determined line, no trace of hesitation, fear or doubt left in her mind. She was filled with new purpose.

Because Charlotte Grant had a plan.

"I shall overlook your indiscretion yesterday night, Charlotte." Hargest's hand gripped the silver top of his walking cane. He seemed more stooped today. He appeared sallow, even a little jaundiced. "Your son is almost five. It will soon be his time to learn his destiny and meet his master."

Charlotte swallowed bile as she saw the old man's rheumy eyes light up. He licked saliva from the corners of his lips. She bit her tongue and said nothing.

"In two nights, he will be brought to you and you will present him in due ceremony to the master. Do you understand?"

Charlotte gave the briefest nod. He mustn't suspect. She must give away nothing.

"You shall have your photograph taken, as a memento for your son to keep. After he is presented, you shall see him no more until he turns sixteen."

Charlotte stared at him. He couldn't seriously believe that she would pose for such a picture or that he would even be alive to know his son at sixteen. The man would be a hundred years old in a few days. On the same day her son turned five.

Hargest's laugh rasped. "I see the disbelief in your eyes. Don't you realize that it doesn't matter whether I am in my body or spirit? I still serve the master who gave me all I desired. All my wealth, position. The power I wielded for all those years. All came from him. I am happy to pay his price."

Charlotte wanted to say so much. All the lives this man had ruined through his cruelty. How many had he sacrificed like the innocent doctor and nurse last night? The beast he served fed on souls, that much was obvious. And ultimately it would take her son's, as it would Hargest's.

Not if she could prevent it. But, for the time being, she had to play the subservient. Bite her tongue, swallow down the bile. Wait. A few more days. Maybe not even that.

The photographer arrived and she posed where Hargest told her. The bowl of fragrant roses seemed incongruous in a house where so much evil reigned. The photographer's hands shook. He couldn't wait to get away from there. Job done, he scurried away, muttering that he would forward his bill. He cast one backward glance at the house, crammed his trilby on his head, balanced his tripod on his shoulder and was gone.

The next night, Charlotte was ready. Hargest had told her that her son would arrive the following morning. This was her only chance. She couldn't afford to get it wrong.

The cook and the maid had left at seven and she was alone in the house with her employer. As usual, he spent the evening in his room. Usually the maid took Hargest's evening whisky up to him before she left for the night, but Charlotte had told her to go early. It was her last day. The maid thanked her and left. She'd given her one-week's notice and the sooner she was gone, the better it obviously suited her. Like so many before her, she had cited her employer's temper and, "He gives me the creeps, Miss."

Charlotte locked the front door and took the tray from the hall table. She had a strange, ethereal feeling, as if she was watching herself mount the stairs, her movements controlled not by her but by some force that had temporarily taken possession of her mind.

She knocked on Hargest's door and a brief growl summoned her to enter.

Inside, the dark Victorian furniture overpowered even the generous proportions of the room. A stuffy, stale atmosphere wrinkled Charlotte's nose and made her long to throw open the windows and let in the fresh, cleansing air.

Hargest looked up as she came toward him. She set the tray down and poured his whisky, added the right quantity of water and handed it to him. His hand shook as he took the glass from her.

No, not long now.

He took a sip. Charlotte stood squarely in front of him. He frowned. Maybe it was the glimmer of a smile on her face. Maybe. But too late. He dropped the glass and clawed at his throat. Then at the air.

Good to know the rat poison was still so effective. Heaven alone knew how long it had been down in that cellar. Hargest tried to stand. He staggered forward. Tried to reach for her, but she stepped back. He fell and the house began to pulsate and pound.

Charlotte snapped out of her trance-like state. In horror, she stared at Hargest's twitching body lying on the floor and the full impact of what she'd done hit her. His lips had turned blue. His breath rattled in his throat. The thumping grew louder, all around her. With a cry, she ran out of the room, down the stairs to the front door. Her trembling fingers wouldn't turn the key. Behind her, footsteps thudded down the stairs. Roars from hell itself shook the house. The key turned. She raced out into the chilly night and made straight for the only place of safety she knew. The tree. Only as she hugged its trunk, did she dare to turn her head toward the house. Lights blazed through the open door. Shadows danced and flickered in a reddish light on the third floor. In that room. Not a glimmer from Hargest's room.

Charlotte's breath fogged in the moonlight. She shivered. A warm blanket of calm enfolded her. The chill night air gave way to a comforting earthiness and a soft carpet of fragrant green willow leaves.

"Nathaniel Hargest's spirit has left his body. It has been claimed."

The sadness in the spirit's voice was more tragic than anything Charlotte had heard before. It frightened her. "But now I can find my son. I can leave Hargest House and—"

"You can never leave Hargest House. Not until you die."

"But he's dead. I killed him."

"And that is why you can never leave Hargest House. And you will never see your son."

Charlotte's tears flowed. Once again, the spirits she could not see took her arms and led her back to the hazy wall that separated her from the cellar.

"I don't understand."

"Charlotte, you have sinned by killing Nathaniel Hargest. His life was not yours to take. Evil is not extinguished because the intention was good. You will have to make a choice. The demon will take a soul."

Charlotte gave way to sobbing. She fell on her knees, her head in her hands. "He cannot take my son. He mustn't. There has to be a way."

"Then you must sacrifice another."

"It can take me. I'm the one who killed Nathaniel Hargest. Let it take me."

"No, Charlotte. It cannot be you. You have committed a mortal sin and you are no longer innocent. Payment must be made with one who is."

"But Hargest wasn't innocent. He murdered so many."

"He paid for his wealth with his soul—and the souls of the innocent. If your son is not forfeit, the demon will accept your sister's daughter. One day, it will send an acolyte to claim her. Until that time, no demons will plague you. The house will be yours and yours alone. You son must never know you, or the demon will come for him."

Charlotte woke on the floor of the cellar, with no recollection of getting there. She stretched stiffened limbs and looked around. She touched the strangely veined wall behind her and flinched as a small electric shock shot up her arm. She stared in disbelief. Somehow, she must have come through that wall. She held out her hands to it once more, daring to touch it. This time no shock deterred her and she stroked the veiny surface. Impossible to think that somehow, through some power of the tree spirits, they could transform this solid wall into something porous enough for her to enter through.

Nothing made any sense anymore. Her head ached and every limb and muscle cried out for rest, but how could she rest in this house of evil? She struggled to her feet and dragged herself up the wooden steps leading to the kitchen.

A draft told her the front door was still open and she staggered into the hall. Ten minutes after she closed the door, the letterbox clattered and a single white envelope fluttered to the floor.

Charlotte retrieved it and saw it was addressed to her. She recognized the handwriting. Marjorie. She unfolded it, but knew what it would say before she began to read the neat, well-formed handwriting.

Dear Charlotte. Maddie is three years old and we have a favor to ask of you. When she is old enough—say seven or so—would you be prepared to take her during the summer holidays? We miss our safaris so much and she is a quiet, well-behaved child. I'm sure she will give you no trouble…

Charlotte laid the letter down and stared out of the window at the drizzle misting the view.

Poor little girl. But I will make sure you enjoy your summers. We shall have such fun together. Until the time comes…

Later, Charlotte went up to her room. She opened her desk drawer and took out her diary and her *Book of Shadows*. There were entries in here that Maddie mustn't find. Incriminating. Frightening even for a little girl and little girls were so inquisitive. They couldn't keep secrets either. And Marjorie would never understand.

Charlotte turned over the pages, re-read the entries and slowly began tearing pages out. She crumpled them up, threw them on the fireplace and struck a match. She waited and watched as the flames licked at the dry paper and her words flew up the chimney and out into the air.

So mote it be.

Maddie

Chapter Sixteen

"What's that tune, Auntie?"

"It's called 'Serenade in Blue', Maddie. Glenn Miller and His Orchestra used to play it a lot during the war. It was one of my favorites. I'll sing it for you…"

Another barrier began to disintegrate in my mind. I clapped my hands to my ears, and squeezed my eyes tight, but I couldn't shut it out. The piano, my aunt singing, the sound drifting up from downstairs.

The song. *That* song. A sentimental forties love ballad. But not on that day. On that day, the sunny memories of my childhood summers ended. And it had all started when Aunt Charlotte played "Serenade in Blue" and the birds stopped singing. Now I remembered. I knew why the sound of it chilled me to the core. The song ended. The phantom piano gave one final flourish and was silent. I opened my eyes. Veronica was gone. Behind me, the creaking began.

The rocking horse, still impossibly standing amid all this devastation. Still moving back and forth on broken rockers.

The door slammed shut.

I screamed.

A fierce cold froze the blood in my veins, as a swirling black mist formed on the far side of the room. A figure began to take shape. I backed away, terrified. I couldn't reach the door. To do so, I would have to go right past that mist.

The mist began to settle and take form. The figure of a man emerged. A tall man in a long black coat, carrying a walking stick with a lion on a silver top. I screamed again. The door flew open.

A familiar figure. Aunt Charlotte looked first at me and then at the man. His face began to dissolve, to change from the figure I recognized as Nathaniel Hargest. I shrank back still farther, until I almost touched the rocking horse. It stopped moving.

Hargest's face lengthened, lost definition. The eyes became blazing fires of red and yellow, the nose disappeared and the mouth opened, to reveal massive, vicious fangs. The gaping maw grew. I screamed and shrank from it.

Aunt Charlotte stepped forward. She pointed at the demon. It bared fangs at her. A loud wheezing, like an orchestra of bellows, echoed around the room.

More figures entered the room. They clustered around Aunt Charlotte. I knew them all. Veronica, Sonia, Thelma, and Tom in his gray pullover. They said nothing, just formed a silent, defiant group as the creature morphed. It reared its head and I saw it was covered in tree roots. Its eyes had sunk into a bark-like trunk, behind masses of writhing, snake-like tendrils.

A scarecrow, Neil had said. This thing would scare a lot more than crows.

Every nerve in my body tensed.

Aunt Charlotte gathered her group of my imaginary siblings closer. As one, they pointed at the beast. It began to fade.

Once it had gone, they turned and, without a glance at me, walked quietly out of the room. Only Aunt Charlotte remained. I opened my mouth to speak, but she silenced me with a finger to her lips.

"Now you will remember," she said, and left me alone.

I have no idea how long I stayed there, trying to understand what had happened. Above all, wondering when those memories would come flooding back to me. And fearing what those recollections would reveal. I didn't have to wait long.

"*The child isn't yours.*"

The voice drifted into my dream. It didn't belong there. I was dreaming of sunshine and a picnic with people I didn't recognize, but in this dream they were my friends. The sun shone, a few puffy clouds drifted across the sky. Birds sang. Champagne glasses clinked. Laughter rang out across the field where we sat on checkered cloths. I reached behind me for more wine. That's when it all changed. Everything stopped. The sky grew black. The people had vanished. My hand held empty space where the bottle should have been.

The familiar woman's voice echoed around me. "The child isn't yours."

I peered through the gloom. I could see nothing.

Some unconscious part of me wrenched myself from my dream. It took me a moment to realize where I was—lying, fully clothed, on my bed at Hargest House with no recollection of leaving the junk room or how much time had passed. Pale moonlight cast shadows in the room. I listened, not daring to move. The voice had sounded so close, so real. Aunt Charlotte's voice. In the distance I heard music and put my hand to my mouth.

"Serenade in Blue".

It drifted up from downstairs. Someone was playing the piano.

I moistened my dry lips and padded barefoot to the door. Out in the corridor the sound of the music was louder. The melody played on. I grasped the banister and began my descent.

I reached the bottom of the stairs. Still the music played.

The door of the living room was slightly ajar. Behind it, the piano played on. I hesitated. Should I throw it open, or try and creep around it? I took a deep breath and pushed.

The door swung back. The room was full of a swirling gray smoke. The piano played on. No one was seated at it. Someone grasped my hand from behind. The familiar voice spoke.

"The child is not yours."

Suddenly I was on the other side of the room, standing next to the piano. It was daylight outside.

The sun streamed through the window as Aunt Charlotte played first "Spanish Eyes" and "Misty". The windows were wide open and birdsong filtered through. An enthusiastic blackbird kept up a constant refrain, so that whenever Aunt Charlotte stopped playing, his pure trill sang his summer song.

The first few notes of "Serenade in Blue" changed everything. She cried out. "No, I won't play that. Why can't I stop?" Her eyes were wide, terrified. "Maddie. I can't stop playing this and I mustn't. Not today. Not anymore. Ever."

"But you told me it's your favorite song."

Aunt Charlotte shook her head. Her face muscles tensed as if she was battling for control. "*No*. It was all right before. When you were younger. But tomorrow is your birthday and it becomes *his* song. It becomes the devil's serenade. I must never play it again. Never. It will bring him here. I thought I'd be able to stop, but I'm playing it. I don't know how… it's not my doing. Please believe me, Maddie. I never wanted any of this. I was so scared."

"But, I don't understand."

Aunt Charlotte's lips were set in a thin line, as she fought to stop playing. I tried to pry her fingers off the keyboard but they refused to move. Her stiff fingers somehow managed to play the melody as beautifully as the composer could ever have wished.

I heard a noise behind me, gagged at the reek of sulfur, and stared at Aunt Charlotte as her fingers finished playing the song and the piano lid crashed down, narrowly missing them.

"Today's the day he comes back."

I spun around. A scream sliced through the air and I realized it was mine. The blackbird stopped singing. All the birds stopped. When the echo of my scream died away, only the wheezing of the thing that had once been Nathaniel Hargest punctuated the unnatural stillness. I looked down at my feet and realized. I recognized the black platform sandals I had saved up for weeks to buy. I was sixteen years old again. Back in that summer. Or remembering it. But I had perfect recall of being my adult self, as if I was possessing my body as a young girl on the day everything changed.

The swirling smoke parted and I gasped. A tall man in a black morning coat and top hat emerged. My adult self knew him instantly. Nathaniel Hargest had returned from his evil underworld.

Aunt Charlotte's voice was strong. "The child is not yours. You shall not take her."

The man's expression turned angry. His eyes flashed red. I shrank closer to my aunt, feeling all the emotions of a teenage girl in danger.

"Why does he want to take me?" My voice didn't sound like it came from me. More like that of a little girl.

He pointed at me and I flinched still farther.

"It is time, Charlotte. You bargained with the master. Your son for her."

"I revoke the bargain," my aunt said and reached under the sheet music on the piano next to her. She brandished the willow wand.

Hargest laughed. "Do you think that will protect her? That trinket?"

He raised his hand and the wand flew out of my aunt's hand. It ignited, and hovered in mid-air. Hargest's laugh rasped and turned to a cry as the burning wand arrowed toward him, piercing his chest. He stumbled and fell to his knees, staring at my aunt in disbelief.

"Never underestimate the forces of the light," Aunt Charlotte said.

A few feet away, Hargest appeared to be recovering. He staggered to his feet. "And you should never underestimate the forces of darkness. They saved you once, from your miserable life. You knew there was a price to pay."

"And I paid it. I have never seen my son. The son you made me bear and took away from me."

Hargest shook his head. "Not I, Charlotte. The master."

Behind Hargest, the smoke swirled again.

My aunt's hand pushed me. "Get behind me, Maddie. Don't look in its eyes. Don't let it see you."

Something was tugging at my mind. Some force pulled me, tried to drag me out of the body of my sixteen-year-old self. The swirling black smoke pulsated and throbbed. A roar shook the house. I crouched down behind Aunt Charlotte and turned my face to the wall.

"The master has come to reclaim his own."

"She does not belong to him." I had never heard Aunt Charlotte speak so forcefully.

"The bargain was clear. On the girl's sixteenth birthday, her life and soul would be forfeit to the master. You were happy for it then."

I couldn't believe what I was hearing. Aunt Charlotte had traded my life and soul for her son. I was too shocked to cry, but despair and terrible loneliness gripped me. The pounding and roaring grew. I crammed my hands against my ears. This couldn't be happening. I would wake soon and find I had dreamed it all.

But I didn't wake up. The stench of sulfur was overpowering and I started to cough.

Hargest laughed.

"He will take her. Tomorrow at the appointed time. He will return."

"She will not be here. She is going away and will never return."

"But, dear Charlotte, that cannot be. She *will* return."

"I have the forces of light to help me."

"They can only hold off the inevitable. If they can even do that."

"No, they are strong and will grow stronger. I will stay here in this house. I will help them grow."

A massive roar silenced my aunt. A sudden rush of heat shot into the room. Instinctively, I looked. A hideous pair of clawed, scaly feet stood a yard or so away. A tail with a snake's head coiled, uncoiled, pounded the ground. I cowered farther back and put my head in my hands. I peered between my fingers. The demon moved forward.

Aunt Charlotte cried out, "Lord and Lady, protect us!"

A strong smell of peaty earth mingled with the stench of sulfur.

Others had joined us. They were chanting in some language I didn't understand. The chanting grew louder. They were moving toward us. The creature roared again.

The house trembled.

My aunt spoke. Despite everything, her voice remained even, controlled. "The tree spirits have shown you what they are prepared to do. It must be enough."

Hargest paused. "The master is pleased. A sacrifice will be made, but he will be generous. You must bring the girl to the place of assembly tomorrow at midnight, but he will not take her. Not this time."

Aunt Charlotte's voice wavered for the first time. "How do I…how do we know that it… he will keep his word?"

"He is the lord and master. Do not doubt him."

The scene melted in front of me and I was outside. The night was chilly. Black. My sixteen-year-old self held my aunt's hand. We stood near the river, a few yards from the tentacle tree. Alone.

"What's happening?" I asked, shivering, though not from cold.

"We must wait, Maddie. You must be very brave."

"But, Aunt, I don't understand. That man said you had a son and that you chose to save him and give me to him instead. I thought you loved me." Tears coursed down my cheeks.

In the gloom I caught the glistening of tears on my aunt's cheek. Her voice quivered. "I do, Maddie. When I made that stupid bargain, I'd never met you. I was so scared. Desperate. I would have done anything to save my son. I offered myself, but I was not pure enough. You came here that first summer and I began to love you as the daughter I had never had. Would never have. I knew I couldn't give you up, so I asked the spirits for help."

"And will they help? What will happen to me if they don't?"

Aunt Charlotte clasped me tight, so I could barely breathe. "They will help us, darling. And you mustn't be frightened when you see them. They…well, they don't look like us. They…"

In the distance, a dog barked. Then it whimpered. Yelps of pain. Silence.

"Good evening, Charlotte."

I jumped. Hargest tipped his hat to us. He seemed as solid and human as my aunt and me. Hard to believe he wasn't a living, breathing soul with a beating heart and blood running through his veins.

"Ah, you have brought company, I see."

For a second, I thought he meant me, until I realized he was looking over my shoulder. A strong smell of peaty earth wafted under my nose. A sound like branches dragging across the ground made me turn. Too late, my aunt tried to stop me. I screamed as three figures like small trees moved. Their faces were elongated, woody. Protruding from their backs, intertwined twigs were woven into wings that could surely never fly. Where their eyes should be, clusters of fireflies danced in almond formations. I could make out no mouths and realized the earthy smell came from these dark green, alien creatures.

Aunt Charlotte held me tightly to her. I couldn't stop whimpering. "Hush. Don't be afraid, my child."

Hargest's voice rasped. "Put her aside, Charlotte."

She released her hold on me and motioned me to stand next to the willow. The tree-like figures parted for me to get through. One stroked my arm with a green tendril. I gave a little cry of fear and crept into the tree's hollow, where I cowered and watched.

Hargest parted his thin lips and a foul stench of sulfur, like a hundred rotten eggs, sent bile washing up into my throat. A thin stream of vomit shot from my mouth and I coughed and choked. I wiped my mouth with the back of my trembling hand.

"The master has accepted the sacrifice. It shall be done. The girl shall live. For now."

Aunt Charlotte's voice was steady and firm. "The debt is being paid by another. One whose soul must be far more valuable to him."

Hargest's smile chilled every pore of my body. "Your son will live. The girl will live. You will leave the house and all your possessions to her. When you are gone, she will inherit Hargest House and all that remains."

"She will never return. Never."

"But we both know she will."

There was a long silence. Hargest broke it. "The master will take your sacrifice."

In front of me two of the tree spirits moved aside. The one in the center—the one who had touched me—began to glow. It started as a pale yellow light deep in the cluster of roots that formed its feet. As it began to burn orange, the other spirits began to chant.

A dark cloud formed around Hargest. His eyes flashed red and yellow flames, his face lengthened and great woody tendrils grew from his arms, legs and torso. They thickened, became branches, scorched black as charcoal. In contrast to the verdant tree spirits, he looked dead. And in that death, lurked evil.

Hargest slithered forward on mulched, rotten roots. He raised his disgusting skeletal branches and cradled the glowing tree spirit in a hideous parody of Klimt's most famous masterpiece. The tree spirit struggled. It made no sound except for the rustling of its limbs. The contrast between it and the evil creature that held it captive couldn't have been more pronounced. Pure good versus pure evil. Yes, I had feared the tree spirits in their natural form, but now, I could appreciate their true beauty, hidden deep within.

With mounting horror, I realized the spirit's glow was waning. Hargest's tree monster was sucking the life and soul out of his victim.

Aunt Charlotte was weeping. Tears streamed down my face too at the sight of the innocent, good spirit that had sacrificed itself for me, and for my aunt's unknown son.

The glow was extinguished. Hargest dropped the cold, blackened, dead husk. It cracked and disintegrated into a cluster of dead twigs. The other tree spirits stood, unmoving.

Hargest was already transforming back into the man.

"This is not finished, Charlotte. It is merely…postponed."

"Your master has taken a great and good soul. A supreme sacrifice. Surely that should sate even that demon's foul appetites long after my niece has lived her life."

Hargest's lips curled in a grimace that became a grating, raucous laugh. "All those years ago you truly thought I selected you because I needed a housekeeper, when in truth, I had searched for you for decades; the woman who would bear my child, and provide my master with the souls he craved. You have done well. I could never have brought him such a prize as you have today."

"It's over."

"The master will want nothing more from you other than you leave the house and contents to the girl. Fail to do that and you will hear from him again."

"It shall be done."

The vision vanished. Something snapped in my brain—like an elastic band stretched too tight. I was back in my own time, crouched on the living room floor, hugging my knees and rocking back and forth.

My muscles ached from sitting rigidly in one position for too long, but I barely noticed the cramping pain. My thoughts were all on the memory that had finally come back to me. Hargest had said I would return. Aunt Charlotte had left the house to me. She knew I would return. And now I was in mortal danger. The supreme sacrifice of the tree spirit had only sated the demon's appetite for a time. It was coming back and, unlike my aunt, I had no bargaining tools.

I must get out of there. I had to run and never look back. I told myself Charlie must have gone without me. I had to escape.

I struggled to my feet and made my labored way to the door. Out in the hall, they were waiting for me. All my imaginary siblings.

Thelma put her hand out to me. "Come with us, Kelly. We'll look after you."

"But you're not real. I made you up."

"We're here to keep you safe," Sonia said.

A small hand tugged at my sleeve. Veronica looked up at me with her bright blue eyes. I took her hand in mine and felt warmth, as if from a real human being, not a product of my overactive imagination.

Tom led the way. Thelma and Sonia came next, then me, holding Veronica's hand.

"Where's Charlie?" I asked.

No answer.

In the kitchen, I drew back as Tom opened the cellar door.

"No, I can't go down there. The tree…"

"It's there to protect you, Kelly." Thelma stroked my cheek. I recoiled. Despite what I had witnessed, my mind still wouldn't allow me to accept that any of it was real. A part of me clung on to the forlorn hope that I was dreaming, having the longest, most frightening nightmare in the history of the world. This couldn't be happening. I couldn't have felt a warm, dry hand caress my face.

"I'm Maddie. My name's Maddie. Kelly's a name I called myself when I was with you."

Tom chuckled. "You're Kelly to us in this form."

"I still can't go down there."

"But you must." Veronica slid her hand out of mine. "It's the only way you can be safe. The only way to protect you from *him*."

"Who?" But I knew the answer before Thelma spoke it.

"Nathaniel Hargest. He has come for you as he said he would."

"That's why I need to get away from here. As far and as fast as possible."

"It won't be far enough or fast enough. He knows where you are. He will find you. This is the only way."

I tried again. "Where's Charlie?"

Tom lit a cigarette. Thelma frowned at him but said nothing. "He's gone."

"Gone? But his van's still there."

"See for yourself."

I looked out of the kitchen window. My car stood outside. Alone.

Tom stood by my shoulder. "See? There's just you and us." He smiled.

Thelma beckoned to me. "Come on now, Kelly. You must go down to the cellar. You'll be safe there."

Her words sounded so final. Is this how it was all going to end? Not without a fight. "No. I'm leaving."

I turned the key in the back door. Tom grabbed my hand and pulled it away. "No, Kelly. You can't do that. Your aunt wouldn't want that. She knew what had to be done. That is why she summoned us. To help you."

Thelma was within a couple of feet of me and I had nowhere else to go. They had formed a semi-circle around me. Behind me was the sink—its cold steel hardness at my back.

Thelma held out her hand to me and I shrank back from her.

"It's time to go down."

They simultaneously took hold of my arms and pulled my reluctant body toward the cellar door.

I struggled. I pushed back with all my strength, digging my heels into a floor I couldn't grip. Veronica and Tom dragged one arm, Sonia and Thelma the other.

The odor of earthy wood and the sound of something rustling and dragging on the ground seeped under the door.

Tom opened it.

"*No!*" My scream tore through the air, so shrill it rang in my ears, but they ignored me. They pushed me onward. Still I dragged my heels. It was pitch black in there. They hadn't switched on the light. Then I realized why it seemed even darker, as the first root wrapped itself around my arm.

"Let me go!"

Thelma gripped my arm tighter as the root secured its hold on me. "Let go, Maddie," she said and I realized she had used my real name. "The tree will protect you and keep you from harm."

She relinquished her hold on me to the tree. Another root snaked along my other arm.

It squeezed my muscles like a blood pressure cuff.

I cried out, one continuous wail. Terror made me lose control and wetness dripped down my legs. My head buzzed. The roots pulled me down the steps. I half turned as Thelma let go my arm and I saw the four "siblings" grouped at the top of the stairs. Through my fear-misted eyes I watched them transform. Human features dissolved into bodies of smooth green bark. Hands and feet became long, slender branches. They became the tree spirits I had seen so recently. Their heads grew tall, crowned with brush and leaves, while from their backs, their wings stood proud.

They were there to protect me from an evil that terrified me so that my screams became raucous cries. But last time they had protected me, one of them had died. I couldn't expect such a sacrifice this time. I had no idea what form their protection would take. I shut my eyes, only to open them again as roots brushed my face and wrapped themselves around it. Before I lost consciousness, "Serenade in Blue" wafted down to me.

The smell of damp earth hung all around me. It took a few moments before I remembered. I opened my eyes, terrified at what I would see. The dim light illuminated unfamiliar surroundings. I sat up. Around me, the walls—if you could call them that—were of bark and encircled the space I was sitting in. I rubbed my eyes. My throat stung, as if I was sickening from a cold or flu. All my screaming had probably damaged my vocal cords. A new fear clutched at me, my stomach contracted and I managed to turn my head away in time before a thin stream of bile projected from my mouth, soaking into the ground next to me and releasing a sour odor.

I wiped my mouth with the back of my hand, but stopped halfway. In the shadows something moved.

"Hello, Maddie, my old friend."

Another barrier dissolved in my head. A new memory played a film reel behind my eyes. A hot summer's day down by the river, playing near the tree. I couldn't have been more than about eight or nine. I'd made a daisy chain and a little boy a couple of years older than me placed it around my wrist. We both laughed. He tagged me and off we ran. Fast forward and a new memory played. The boy and me, older. That last summer. It had to be. By the tentacle tree. My first kiss. But darkness had shut out the sun. The birds had stopped singing.

The smile had frozen on the boy's face. "Don't turn around, Maddie. Don't look behind you. Look at me. Look at me."

But I had turned around. I had seen what he saw. A man, but not a man. Eight feet tall. Two glinting green eyes where the head should be, but where an elliptical mass of twisted bark perched on shoulders of intertwined branches that tapered into long, slender twigs. The creature's mouth was a knot of wood that opened to reveal blackness within. The torso was formed from gnarled and twisted branches that extended into two distinct trunks, each covered with bark. As it shuffled forward, it trailed yet more branches, while roots concealed where feet should have been.

I couldn't move. I couldn't even cry out. I knew this thing couldn't be there. But it was. The boy had seen it too. The memory stopped abruptly as if a reel of cine film had snapped. I knew who my companion was.

"Charlie. It was you, wasn't it? All those years ago? You warned me about the… About Hargest."

The figure moved out of the shadows. Incredibly, he was smiling.

"Hello again, Maddie."

I struggled to my feet. "I didn't remember any of it. Our childhood friendship. That last summer…"

He drew me to him for a comforting hug.

"When did you remember?" he asked.

"Just now. My memory of my sixteenth birthday has been coming back to me since yesterday, I think. I'm not sure. I've lost track of time. But I had a vision of Aunt Charlotte fending off Hargest…and the tree sprits protected me. One died…" My voice tailed away.

Charlie held me tighter. His heartbeat quickened. "When I first came to the house and you answered the door, you looked familiar, but I couldn't place you. A few days ago, everything fell into place. The strange dreams I kept having all through my childhood. Occasionally even now. Dark dreams."

A sudden fear gripped me. I pulled away so I could look into his eyes. "Why should you have dark dreams, Charlie? What haven't you told me?"

He took a deep breath. "I'm her son. Your Aunt Charlotte's. My father was Nathaniel Hargest."

My mouth dropped open and I made no attempt to close it. Charlie looked as if he wanted to be anywhere but where we stood. But once started, he had to tell me everything.

"I found out a few days ago. I always knew I was adopted, but when I told my mother I was working for you, she broke down. I had never seen her sob like that. Not even when my father died. She told me about Hargest's coven. How she and my father—the man I always called my father—had been his most loyal followers. That's why Hargest gave me to them. Their loyalty was beyond question. She told me about the ancient demons that have haunted Priory St. Michael for centuries. The black dog that haunts the High Street, born of a she-devil and slave to Zebullas—the demon that Hargest and his coven worshiped. When the coven was disbanded, its members became disillusioned. The demon gave them nothing in return for their devotion. Only Hargest benefited—and he got the lot. Riches, power. Freedom from the poor upbringing he despised so much."

"And Aunt Charlotte never found out where you were."

"Hargest swore them to secrecy and threatened them with demonic revenge if they ever revealed my true identity. Even now, my mother's scared she shouldn't have told me. Soon after Hargest died, my father contracted cancer. He was given a few months to live. My mother was at her wits' end and one day she wandered into the parish church, knelt down and prayed. The vicar saw her there. He prayed with her and she told me she had a vision. The stained-glass window with the picture of St. Michael came alive. There, before her eyes, he slew the dragon. She fainted and when she came round, the vicar was holding her hand. She told him what she had seen and, although he didn't tell her, she knew he'd seen the same vision as she had. A month later, my father was pronounced clear of the cancer that had stricken him. He died thirty-five years later."

I swallowed. "So you weren't raised as a devil worshiper?"

Charlie smiled and shook his head. "Far from it. Church every Sunday morning and Sunday school in the afternoon. I was even a Boy Scout. Got the badges to prove it."

He grew serious again. "Last night, I couldn't sleep. I got up to make a hot drink and, from out of nowhere, memories flooded back of that summer when you were sixteen and I had just turned eighteen. I remembered how beautiful you looked in the sunshine, down by the river. I had to kiss you. Couldn't help myself. Of course, back then, I had no idea we were related. But then…it…appeared. I tried to protect you, but you saw it. You ran away screaming and I never saw you again. Until you answered the door a few weeks ago. "

That was it. The last piece of the infernal jigsaw. I tried to take it all in. Charlie, my old summer friend. My cousin! Hard to take in as I'd imagined then we would become boyfriend and girlfriend. But that all ended that dreadful summer. More memories drifted back into my mind. My mother screaming, hurling abuse at Aunt Charlotte. My father having to restrain her, holding her arms so she couldn't hit her sister, who already had a bleeding and swelling eye where a paperweight had sliced her eyebrow.

I had watched the tirade as if through a veil. I'd curled into fetal position on Aunt Charlotte's settee as it all came back to me. My parents had been summoned back early from their safari. Snatches of the terrible row I had suppressed in my mind for so long returned to me.

My mother crying, "What have you done to her?"

Aunt Charlotte standing there. Silent. Her eyes closed as if in prayer.

"Answer me, you *bitch*. The doctor said she was in shock. Something terrible happened. Something so terrible, her brain has shut down. She could be like this for weeks. Months. Maybe…"

My father trying to comfort her. "Hush, Marjorie. You'll make yourself ill."

My mother choking back sobs. "You'll never see her again…do you hear me, bitch? *Never*. From now on, we are dead to you. Dead. You don't contact us. You don't come near us."

They didn't take me home at first.

"I ended up in some sort of sanatorium I suppose. I'd blocked that from my mind too, but now I remember a procession of doctors and nurses, needles, and drugs to keep me from feeling anything. Afterwards I didn't remember anything about that summer. But there were some anomalies. Like, I could never listen to Glenn Miller again. I never realized why until now."

Charlie took my hand and I became aware again of our surroundings. Still holding his hand, I looked around. "Where are we?"

"Haven't you guessed?"

I shook my head.

"The tree. It's protecting us."

I stared at him. "Are you seriously telling me we are inside that willow tree by the river? Are you crazy?"

Charlie held me at arm's length. His eyes burned into mine. "You have to understand, your Aunt Charlotte has done everything she can to protect you from Hargest's evil. She's trying to put right the terrible wrong she did, even from beyond the grave. That's why she sent *them*. She thought they might comfort you."

"If, by 'them' you mean the imaginary family I created, they frightened the bloody life out of me. Then the first time I saw them as they really are…"

"Like a pure version of Hargest. But still scary. They are elemental spirits. They've walked this earth since before time, their form and ability to move between dimensions is alien to us because it's not something we humans are prepared for. It's beyond our understanding but, in time…"

"So do we become like them? Do we die?"

Charlie shrugged. "I don't have any answers either. And there's something else." He shook his head. "Something I don't understand yet…"

His voice tailed off and I stared at him. The searing pain of fear had been almost swamped by the revelations Charlie had shared with me. Now, though, the terror flooded back. "My God, Charlie, how do we get out of here?"

He put his arm around me and drew me close. "For now, we don't. We wait."

"For what?"

Charlie sighed. "I haven't a clue."

We sat together on the dirt floor, each wrapped up in our own thoughts. My body overflowed with unshed tears, but my eyes—like his—remained dry. My emotions were too tautly strung to spill out in the relief of sobbing.

I glanced at my watch, but it had stopped. Stuck at twelve fifteen. I guessed that must have been the exact time I had been transported here. Wherever "here" was. I could hear nothing, except a distant creaking, as if of branches swaying in a stiff breeze. Were we really in the tree itself? Or had it created some sort of protective shield around us in the cellar? I had no answers, only question after question, while hopeless despair gnawed at my gut.

Maybe through exhaustion, or through the exercise of some strange force, I fell asleep…

Chapter Seventeen

...and awoke with a start. My mind was in a fog. For a second I couldn't think where I was. Slowly, the mist cleared. Somehow, I was lying on the settee in my living room and Shona was bending over me. Her frown transformed into a smile as I blinked at her.

"Where's Charlie?" I said and drew myself up.

"At home I should imagine. It's six o'clock. I didn't expect to find you here, but I came early to get things ready for tonight's rehearsal. Are you all right? You're so pale."

I improvised. "I had the strangest dream," I said, but stopped short of telling her about it.

Shona's eyes bored into me. I looked away, fearful she could read my thoughts somehow and guess the truth.

She sat down opposite me. "I didn't think you were ever coming back here."

"I wasn't." I swung my legs over onto the floor and rubbed my eyes. Yet again, I hadn't a clue how I'd got there. More tricks, bending dimensions or whatever it was the tree spirits did? "I don't even understand what I'm doing here. Except I went to look for Charlie..." My voice faded as I caught Shona's continuing intense gaze. I broke eye contact.

"I was going to make a coffee," she said. "Would you like one?"

"Yes, please. It might help."

She left me alone with my muddled thoughts. When she returned five minutes later, I was still no clearer on what I had experienced. I had no memory of lying down on the settee and all the thoughts in my head were of Charlie and me in that strange place. Somehow, impossibly, within that tree.

Shona handed me a mug of coffee and I set it down on the small table next to me. I could never take my drinks boiling hot.

She sat opposite me and sipped hers, then pointed at my mug. "You want to get that down you. Perk you up."

I tried a feeble smile. "Why? Have you put a little something in it?"

She choked, coughing and spluttering, as tears streamed down her face.

"Are you okay? Did it go down the wrong way?"

She nodded, still unable to speak, still coughing. Something wasn't right about her behavior since I had woken up. It bothered me. I suppose I'll never be sure of any more than that, why I decided to sniff my drink before tasting it. Maybe I was expecting a whiff of brandy, or alcohol of some other kind.

I didn't expect the distinctive aroma of bitter almonds.

Shona was preoccupied with wiping her streaming eyes on a tissue. She didn't see me wrinkle my nose. When I "accidentally" knocked the mug over, she leaped to her feet.

"I'll go and get a cloth," she said.

"No need," I said. "I'll get one. Later."

"But it'll stain," she said.

"I'm sure it will," I said. "But why should I care? I'm leaving here anyway."

She stared at me. And, at that moment, I knew she realized I'd guessed.

"Why, Shona? Who are you really?"

But, of course, by then I had worked it out.

Her short black hair grew down her back; the woman toppled onto all fours, the seams of her smart navy suit stretched and split and her hair became a glossy coat of fur. I backed away, heading for the door as her eyes flashed red. Canine teeth sprouted from her rapidly lengthening snout and a low rumbling growl bounced off the walls.

I had to get out of there before her transformation was complete. I made it outside, just as I heard the stomping of paws behind me. I slammed the front door shut and there was a splintering crash as the huge black dog made contact with the heavy wood. Several of the glass panels shattered and a massive black paw scrabbled through the hole. My car stood outside, but I didn't have my keys.

I ran down the drive. A white van hurtled toward me, its brakes screeching as the driver pulled up inches from me.

"Maddie. Get in!" Charlie threw open the passenger door and I scrambled inside, barely aware of what I was doing.

The tires squealed as he spun the wheel and made off. Behind us, the animal had made it through the door and was charging after the van. Charlie shot out onto the High Street, narrowly missing a lorry. The angry horn blasts faded into the distance, and we sped up the street, past the apartments and out of the town.

Only then dared I draw a complete breath.

I glanced over at Charlie. His knuckles were white as he gripped the steering wheel, turning the van right and left down narrow country lanes.

"Where are we going?"

"To the only place you'll be safe."

"I'll be safe anywhere but here."

"No you won't."

"I only know that before I came here, I was fine. I had a normal life. I can have that again. Take me away from here, Charlie. *Please*." I had never begged for anything so hard in my life, but his blank expression meant I had no idea if he had even heard me.

Charlie turned the van once more and we were driving over a field. My head kept hitting the roof as the vehicle bumped and struggled over the uneven ground. Charlie spoke and his voice was emotional. Full of regret. "No, Maddie. You can never have that again. I'm so sorry."

"She tried to poison me. Shona. She put cyanide in my coffee. I smelled it. Bitter almonds. And then she changed. She…"

"I knew her—or one of her kind—as Suzannah."

"I've heard that name before."

"Back when the social club was still here, she posed as a barmaid but really she was a cambion—a creature that is neither human nor spirit, but an evil spawn of both that can change shape at will. In her case, Suzannah could transform into a black dog. I remember how it was on the night of the unholy fire. That dog—the one Shona became—it will hunt you down, and through it, Nathaniel will find you and bring you to his master. It's already killed at least once. That poor old woman, Mrs. Lloyd. I'm certain she didn't simply die of a heart attack. She died of fright. I think she guessed what Shona really was and confronted her."

His face contorted and he slammed on the brakes. The van screeched to a halt. My seatbelt stopped me from being thrown through the windscreen, but my ribs hurt like hell.

"Charlie!"

He thumped his head on the steering wheel. He looked at me with reddened eyes, tears streaming down his face, but something in those eyes scared me.

"I'm so, so sorry, Maddie. I'm sorry I ran away and left you in the house on your own. I saw you come out, looking for me, and I hid. When you'd gone, I drove off. I was so scared. He got to me, Maddie. Hargest. At the house. He got inside my head. But I had to come back. I have to do this while I still can. Before he takes over."

Nathaniel Hargest. Reborn in the son? A chill spread through my body. "No, Charlie, no. You're Aunt Charlotte's son too. Call on her. She saved you before, remember? She can save you again."

"No, he's too strong. I tricked them. The spirits. I told them who I was and made them believe I needed protection too. That's why they let me be with you in the tree, but they found out. They sensed what was growing inside me. I know you can't remember. They blanked your memory. They were going to cast me out, but I took you with me. I had to do it. He made me."

I stared at him, horrified. Tears flowed freely down Charlie's face. "I can feel him growing. Like a cancer. In my brain. In my very soul. I have to end this, but you…I have to make sure you're safe. For all time. He must not have you. Charlotte was wrong to trade you for me. She failed anyway. All she did was buy time. He is too powerful."

A soft tapping came from the window behind my head.

Charlie nodded toward the sound. "Go with them. They will protect you. I'll give him what he wants. You'll be safe then."

"No, Charlie. You can't do this! I won't let you die!" I let go my feelings for him. The love I refused to acknowledge, but which had been hidden inside me since a warm summer day so many years ago.

Charlie raised eyes that already held a hellish flame.

Tom spoke to me. "Time to leave. You must come with us. Before it is too late."

A powerful rotting smell invaded my nostrils and I fumbled for the door catch. Many hands took my arms. Tom, Thelma, Sonia, and Veronica reached inside and helped me out. I realized where we were. Charlie had driven around in an elaborate circle. We were back under the willow. Over by the house, the black dog paced up and down. It stopped, sniffed the air and looked over to me. Our eyes met for a second, and I looked into reflections of pure evil.

That was the moment of resignation. Some might call it my epiphany. I had lost Charlie as certainly as I had lost my old life. I could never go back. I took one last look at him. Already, the flame in his eyes was growing stronger. Soon he wouldn't be able to contain it.

"Goodbye, Charlie."

"Goodbye, Maddie." But his voice sounded different. More gruff. More like the long-ago voice that had chilled that summer day in my sixteenth year. When "Serenade in Blue" became the devil's serenade.

I let my imaginary siblings lead me. They took my arms and steered me to the tree. They showed me how to place my hands on the bark and lean into it and when I was safely cocooned inside, they led me to the place I remain. My physical body floated down the river. Maybe it was found. Maybe it drifted out to sea. Food for the fishes. I have no need of it now. My spirit moves easily between the dimensions, although I can never be as my companions are.

I'm safe here. He can't get me—not in the dimension I inhabit—but I can never move out of it. I'm not lonely because my friends keep me company. They appear as themselves, in all their natural beauty.

With their help, I can see what is happening in the world around me. It's as if I watch it through a mist or fine gauze. They have taught me so much. Especially about this house, about Hargest and his evil. Long ago, the willow tree grew with forces of good and evil at its roots. The night it was struck by lightning, the evil escaped. It needed a host and found a willing one in the young Nathaniel Hargest. The boy worked at the mill downriver, sweeping floors day and night for pennies. Every night he went to bed hungry, but when he welcomed the evil spirit into his body and pledged his soul to it, his fortunes changed.

He took the evil into the house he built, even supervising the manufacture of the bricks so he could weave demonic power into the fabric of the building. But the good in the tree remained strong, and reached out with its roots. It couldn't destroy the demon and its acolytes, but it could contain them. At least a little. Enough to save my soul, and my aunt's. She passed over long ago. I don't know when, or if, my time will come to move toward the light that is, so far, shielded from me.

My concept of time has vanished. I have no idea how long I have been here. The long empty, unloved house is up for sale. I died to the world outside without leaving a will so, with no relatives to stake a claim, my property will have been repossessed by the State. I suppose they'll sell it one day. They're certainly trying, but people come and go. No one wants to take on such a big venture, especially now the roof is falling in.

Today something disturbing is happening. A couple are viewing the house. She is pregnant. I feel the unborn presence. My spirit friends are restless. They tell me something is different this time. And I can feel it too. The couple love the house. They want to buy it.

So far I have felt them, but not seen them. My spirits help me soar up from the cellar, unnoticed except that the young woman brushes her ear. Maybe she has felt me, like baby breath. I see the backs of the couple. He is much older than her. The smartly dressed estate agent is expounding the virtues of the dilapidated house. He couldn't care less about these people as long as he gets his commission.

"I'll leave you to have a wander around," he says, at last. "I'll nip outside for a smoke. My only vice." He laughs. I've heard that line from him and his predecessors a hundred times before. These days, I don't even crack a smile.

When the estate agent has gone, the man turns and I gasp. I am unprepared for an encounter with my ex-husband. Neil has aged. But I remind myself I have no idea how much time has elapsed. From the look of him he could be twenty years older than when I last saw him. His receding hair is white, but his suit is expensive, his shoes, highly polished black leather. The watch is, if I'm not mistaken, a Rolex. Neil has come into money.

"So, what do you think, Heather darling? Do you think you could be happy here?"

She's a pretty little thing. All blonde hair extensions, designer mini-skirt and fluttering eyelashes. Oh…and the baby bump. She really shouldn't be wearing five-inch heels when she's carrying all that. It must be due anytime soon. So my ex-husband has bagged himself a trophy wife young enough to be his granddaughter.

She speaks in her Barbie-clone voice. Her voice is tragically eager. "Oh yes, I can't wait, Neily baby. Let's buy it today and it'll be ours before the baby is born."

Neil puts his arms around her and kisses her fully on the lips. She giggles. "We're going to be so happy here. I'll make it so pretty."

"I'm sure you will, Heather, darling. I'm sure you will. I came here once before you know. When the previous owner lived here."

"Really?" His young wife looks around and wrinkles her nose at the dusty, mildewed smell. "That must have been a long time ago."

"It was. She was my ex-wife actually."

"Oh." Heather's lips turn down.

Neil laughs. "She threw me out, but I was glad to go. I really thought I'd seen something horrible in the downstairs toilet."

Heather giggles. I can see which direction her mind works.

"No, not that, silly girl." Neil can still be condescending. "It must have been the Prozac I was on at the time, giving me hallucinations. I thought I saw some horrible monster. It scratched me. I told Maddie and that's when she threw me out."

Heather giggles again. She probably does that a lot.

"She did me a favor anyway. If I'd stayed with her, I would never have cracked that Saudi contract and you, my little darling, wouldn't be the wife of a rich and successful businessman."

Neil grasps her around the waist and I feel as nauseous as I am now capable of. *Well, good for you, Neil.*

"I reckon we'll bag ourselves a bargain at that auction. She had some good stuff here—ornaments and so on. It all comes with the house, so we'll make a tidy sum out of that alone. There's no reserve on this place. I mean, who else would want it in this condition?"

Good old Neil, still counting the cost and calculating the profit.

The estate agent has finished his cigarette.

"Have you seen all you want to see?"

Neil takes a long, hard look around the hall. He hasn't moved into any of the rooms. Heather has been running from the kitchen to the living room, dining room, library, and is on the third stair. But she does what she's told, that one.

"Oh yes," Neil says. "We've seen everything we need to see. Come along, Heather."

The estate agent leads the way out, followed by the girl. Neil brings up the rear. The others have gone slightly ahead. He pauses at the door and turns around.

From far away, a piano begins to play the song I had hoped never to hear again. My friends lay their spirit hands on my shoulders—their touch impossibly warm and gentle.

Neil looks straight at me. A moment of panic. Can he see me?

A smile creeps over his face and his eyes flash a red flame that sends me reeling. "I'll bring them back."

He closes the door.

I hear it at the same time as the others. A sigh, running through the entire fabric of the house.

Hargest has heard him.

And his master is hungry.

About the Author

Following a varied career in sales, advertising and career guidance, Catherine Cavendish is now the full-time author of a number of paranormal, ghostly and Gothic horror novels and novellas.

Her novels include: *Those Who Dwell in Mordenhyrst Hall, The After-Death of Caroline Rand, Nemesis of the Gods, Dark Observation, In Darkness, Shadows Breathe, The Garden of Bewitchment. The Haunting of Henderson Close, The Devil's Serenade, The Pendle Curse* and *Saving Grace Devine.*

The Crow Witch and Other Conjurings is a collection of her previously published and brand new short stories.

Her novellas include: *The Darkest Veil, Linden Manor, Cold Revenge, Miss Abigail's Room, The Demons of Cambian Street, Dark Avenging Angel, The Devil Inside Her,* and *The Second Wife*

She lives by the sea in Southport, England with her long-suffering husband, and a black cat called Serafina who has never forgotten that her species used to be worshipped in ancient Egypt. She sees no reason why that practice should not continue.

You can connect with Cat here:

Website: catherinecavendish.com/
Facebook: facebook.com/CatherineCavendishWriter
X (formerly Twitter): twitter.com/Cat_Cavendish
Instagram: instagram.com/catcavendish/
Tik Tok: catcavendish
Bluesky @catcavendish.bsky.social

Curious about other Crossroad Press books? Stop by our website:
http://crossroadpress.com
We offer quality writing
in digital, audio, and print formats.

Subscribe to our newsletter on the website homepage and receive a free eBook.